David Tasker

Musings of leisure hours

David Tasker

Musings of leisure hours

ISBN/EAN: 9783337086107

Printed in Europe, USA, Canada, Australia, Japan

Cover: Foto ©Andreas Hilbeck / pixelio.de

More available books at **www.hansebooks.com**

MUSINGS OF LEISURE HOURS.

MUSINGS

OF

LEISURE HOURS.

BY DAVID TASKER.

'The autumn leaf is sear and dead ;
It floats upon the water's bed :
I would not be a leaf, to die
Without recording sorrow's sigh.'

KIRKE WHITE.

CARLISLE:
HALSTEAD & BEATY,
CITY STEAM PRINTING WORKS.
1878.

PREFACE.

———◆———

MANY words are unnecessary. In the following rhymes the Author makes no pretensions to poetical abilities. He has merely endeavoured to express in simple language the fancies that would arise in his mind during the intervals of a toil spent amidst the dust and din of the mills and factories since he was twelve years of age. His educational advantages have been necessarily limited, but he does not mention this to disarm criticism. If there is genuine merit in the work, it will command attention ; if not, let it sink, as the Author anticipates it will, into the 'cold shades of oblivion.'

ALLENWOOD, CARLISLE,
   June 20, 1878.

CONTENTS.

———

GLEANINGS FROM NATURE.

PATHETIC MUSINGS.

MISCELLANEOUS RHYMES.

BALLADS, LIVELY AND SERIOUS.

LYRICAL RHYMES.

Gleanings from Nature.

SUNSET.

I SIT by the open casement,
　　The evening is calm and mild,
The summer winds come sighing soft
　　As the breath of a little child,
Wafting into my parlour cool
　　A richly-sweet perfume,
From the lily-oak and the milk-white thorn,
　　And the rosy apple bloom.

God's earth is serenely smiling, clad
　　In the beauties of flowery May ;
The day-king, throned in his crimson car,
　　Sinks grandly far away ;
His slanting beams all quivering fall
　　In a radiant glory rain,
Tinging the woods with a purple sheen,
　　While luminous glows the plain.

Away far over the pleasant fields,
　　Through the dazzling sunset haze,

The grand old hills, in a pale-blue line,
  Break dim on my wandering gaze,
Soaring away 'midst the calm white clouds,
  That sparkle pure and bright,
Like snow-clad amber isles in a sea
  Of golden azure light.

The lowing cattle are roaming glad
  By the brook in the grassy glade,
Which glances bright as a chain of gold
  O'er an emerald carpet laid ;
And the voices of happy children,
  At play on the village green,
With the song-birds' notes all merrily ring
  Through the balmy, blue serene.

God's glory is over all, below
  And above ; while waxeth glad
My heart, that a little while ago
  Throbbed wearily and sad.

———o———

GLOAMING.

THE god of day
Hath sunk away
Behind the far-seen hills ;
The air is calm
As a breath of balm,
The wide expanse which fills.

GLOAMING.

The rosy blush
And the saffron flush,
The pearly clouds that fringed,
Grow dim and pale,
And the emerald vale
With gold no more is tinged.

Like a purple pall,
All gloomily fall
The shadows of eventide ;
The song of the bird
No more is heard
Re-echoing far and wide.

The children that played
- In the lime tree's shade
On the village green, at the call
Of their mothers, have hied
To their homes beside :
Deep silence reigns o'er all.

Like a fairy canoe,
Down the calm, clear blue
Of the western heavens afar,
The night's pale queen
Is sailing serene,
With the sweet-faced gloaming star.

Like angel eyes
From the sapphire skies,
The God-lit lamps peer dim,
Whilst the planets march
Through the measureless arch,
All chanting creation's hymn.

B

And the star-kissed hills,
And the woods and rills,
With the mighty chorus ring ;
All, all proclaim
The glory and name
And might of eternity's King.

——— o ———

AN AUGUST SUNSET AT TALKIN TARN.

THE west wind, balmy and sweet, is hushed,
The wavelets have rocked themselves to rest,
The ambient ether is rosily flushed
Where Sol hangs over the mountain's crest.

Far through the limitless azure dome,
The fleecy cloudlets are drifting slowly,
Like white-robed messengers flying home
To God, from man, on a mission holy.

Warmly the joyous sunlight streams
Along the vale in an amber flow ;
Grandly the yellowing grain-field gleams,
Redly the sombre woodlands glow.

Blue and tranquil the lone mere lies,
Asleep in the radiantly-rosy tide,
Mirroring clearly the sapphire skies,
And the great green hills on the farther side.

But the day-god's parting smiles anoint
With glory the far-seen hills, that kiss

The gold-rimmed clouds, while to me they point
   To a purer and holier home than this.

Now Sol hath sunk in his fiery car,
   The sunset glories have waxen pale,
The lone mere mirrors a new-born star,
   And over all floats a dusky veil.

———o———

THE APPROACH OF SUMMER.

SHE comes, the sweetly-beauteous, blushing maid,
In all her gorgeous loveliness arrayed,
      To cheer us once again ;
Comes from her home, where, 'neath calm, rosy skies,
The olive blooms, and graceful palm trees rise
      In splendour o'er the plain.

Around her tresses, dark as the raven's wing,
Are wreathed, in all their glory blossoming,
      Pale pink and purple flowers ;
Her soft eyes glancing like the stars of night,
Aflash with rays of hope and love, to light
      Her long, bright, joyous hours.

She comes, her balmy influence to impart,
To soothe the weary, sorrow-stricken heart,
      And comfort those that mourn
For lost beloved ones ; her glad, cheering smile
Shall raise their drooping spirits, sad erewhile :
      Again hope shall return.

Come, then, pretty smiling maiden
  From the southern vine-clad hills,
With the balm all richly laden,
  That sad hearts with gladness fills.

——o——

SUMMER COME.

Thou'rt come, and Winter's chill, dark days have fled
  At thy approach, with all their memories sad ;
And Nature, that awhile seemed cold and dead,
  Is smiling now, in all her greenery clad.

And richly-perfumed flowers, of loveliest hue,
  In wild profusion gem the lush, green wold ;
Sweet violets ope their eyes of sparkling blue,
  And buttercups their golden hearts unfold.

Wee daisies blossom, crimson-fringed and white,
  Like snowflakes sprinkled o'er the fallow plain ;
And green leaves, gladd'ning to the heart and sight,
  With all their sunny memories, bloom again.

And all are glad.   The pale-faced ones that sweat
  In the close factories, where they weave and spin,
In idle hours seek some cool, green retreat,
  Far from the city's smoke, and dust, and din ;

And joyous climb the breezy, ferny hills,
  All summering in the blessed sun's glad rays ;
Or roam beside love-hallowed rippling rills,
  Whilst myriad song-birds chant their amorous lays.

They feel the bracing air, perfumed with flowers,
   Refresh their toil-worn limbs and fevered brains :
Then welcome, Summer ! thy calm, rosy hours
   Make weary hearts forget their toils and pains.

——o——

SUMMER.

LIKE a tyrant king from his tottering throne,
Grim Winter has fled to the Frigid Zone,
To reign supreme 'midst his icy cells,
Where the white bear prowls and the walrus dwells;
And dear young Summer now reigneth queen,
Awakening smiles where tears have been.

She has come from that mystical, balmy land
Of dark-eyed maidens and vine-hills grand,
Where beautiful rivers, all sparkling, lave
Green shores ; where the olive and almond wave,
With the orange, and myrtle, and palm tree high,
'Neath the golden blue of a cloudless sky.

In glory she walks through the land unseen,
Adorning the woods with a leafy screen,
Mantling the meadows with loveliest hues,
Nursing the wild-flowers with diamond dews,
And dipping the new-born star-bright bells
In the rich quintessence of fragrant smells.

Now, toil-sick and weary, I long to stray
To the emerald valleys and plains, away

From the populous town, with its dust and din,
Its misery, crime, and disease, and sin,
With Nature communion sweet to hold,
'Midst her marvellous beauties manifold ;

To clamber the breezy, broom-clad hills,
By the mossy margins of tinkling rills,
That with rainbow-tinted lustre glow,
As in miniature cascades they dance and flow
Down their rocky channels, by bosky dell,
And tangled thicket, and fern-clad fell ;

And cull the blue violet and cowslip bright,
The lily pale and wee daisy white,
Under the whispering green-haired pines,
While the sunbeams, slanting in golden lines
Through the cool, dim twilight, all tremulous dart,
Like rays of joy on a sorrowful heart.

Dear Summer, while roaming thy vales and hills,
A dreamy gladness my being fills ;
The sound of the brook and the sigh of the breeze,
The stir in the leaves and the hum of the bees,
The low of the herds and the song of the birds,
Wake feelings within me too deep for words.

———0———

NIGHTFALL.

BEYOND the dim blue mountains,
Far in the west, pale grows
The line of purple daylight,
As night in silence throws

Its weird and gloomy mantle
  O'er all, while sink to rest
Forms with the long day's toiling
  All weary and opprest.

The scattered rows of lamplights
  The seaport that illume,
Like bright-red stars in the distance,
  Gleam through the deepening gloom ;

While sounds of the sailors' voices,
  From the harbour rising, come
Through the breezeless autumn evening
  In a dreamy, fitful hum,

Blending dim with the murmurs
  Of the lone, mysterious sea,
On the shingly beach low splashing,
  Not far away from me.

Now from its broad blue bosom,
  So solemnly serene,
Emerges, calm and beautiful,
  The night's pale, lovely queen ;

Slowly, silently scaling
  The orient azure walls,
While the stars wax pale in her glory,
  And hide in the heavenly halls.

The rippling waves are sparkling
  With a luminous silvery sheen,
While a misty, mellow radiance
  Floats over the tranquil scene.

And over my soul comes stealing,
  Like the moonlight over the main,
A mystical, hallowed feeling,
  That words cannot explain.

————()————

JUNE.

June's golden hours have come again,
  The world looks freshly fair ;
Full sweetly bloom the hawthorn buds,
  And balmy is the air.

Spring flowers now blossom, richly flushed
  With purple, pink, and gold,
Like jewels gleaming over all
  The verdant summer wold.

The tiny-tufted lark is up,
  And singing a merry song
To the amber-tinted clouds that sail
  So silently along.

And rosy-cheekèd children now,
  With gladsome hearts, are seen
Chasing the bee and butterfly
  Over the daisied green.

The smiling hills and waving trees,
  And grain-fields green and grand,
The singing rills and sighing breeze,
  Bespeak a bounteous hand.

And in the golden sunlight
  Of the long, sweet summer day,
Our hearts forget the griefs and cares
  In life's great weary way.

———o———

MORNING.

I LOVE from the town to ramble
  At the dawn of a summer morn,
By the clover meadows and hedgerows,
  And the long, green, dewy corn ;

When the lark from its nest is springing
  With a joyous burst of song,
Ere the sons of labour have wakened
  To the cares that to life belong ;

When the silent, pale night-watchers,
  Afar in the azure deep,
Their eyelids wearily winking,
  In God's arms fall asleep ;

When the dewy wayside flowers
  Ope their tender petals wide, ·
To the day-king grandly rising
  Far over the restless tide.

Oh, then what marvellous changes
  O'er the features of Nature play,
From the first red streak of the dawning,
  To the full, clear light of day !

I think, while I gaze on the landscape,
  With its glory and music and mirth,
Of the bliss for the just hereafter,
  If heaven be fairer than earth.

———o———

NOON.

I LOVE abroad to ramble
  In the noontide's sultry hour,
And to lie beside a river
  In a cool, green, leafy bower ;

Overhead the drooping branches
  By the summer wind soft swayed,
And their pleasant rustling blending
  With the dreamy murmur made

By the silv'ry lambent river,
  Rippling gently to the sea,
And the birds' sweet, merry music,
  And the humming of the bee.

Then a feeling, strange and dreamlike,
  O'er my yearning spirit steals,
Of a mingled joy and sadness,
  Which no other time reveals.

———o———

NIGHT.

THE hamlet is hushed in slumber,
 The hour is starry and still,
On this April night, while I linger
 Alone on a lonely hill.

The cool winds sigh so softly,
 That the leaves are scarcely stirred,
And o'er the gloom-veiled landscape
 No living sound is heard ;

But only the brook's low murmur,
 And the clock in the old church tower
That solemnly, through the stillness,
 Proclaimeth the passing hour.

Now feelings so calm and soothing
 Over my senses steal,
For my mind is filled with the glory
 God's infinite works reveal.

Yes, awe and wonder and worship
 All mingle within my soul,
Beholding those regions supernal,
 Where, under His wise control,

Planets and stars stupendous
 In silence their rounds pursue,
With systems in endless order,
 Hidden from mortal view

The vaulted, mystical chambers
  Of heaven's eternal King,
Adorned with their countless jewels,
  Divinely glittering,

Beyond all sights resplendent,
  Beyond all words sublime,
To me they are ever pointing
  Beyond the grave and time.

———o———

LONGINGS FOR THE COUNTRY.

MOTHER, come, let us be going
  Away from the sultry town ;
No cool winds here are blowing,
  And the air with smoke is brown.
My heart is heavy and weary,
  My bosom with many a sigh
Is heaving ; the days seem dreary,
  And the hours go slowly by.

The spring-time, mother, is ended,
  The joyous summer is come ;
And oh, how I long to spend it
  Where the busy brown bees hum,
'Midst the wild-flowers sweetly growing
  All over the emerald down,
Where the breezes pure come blowing,
  And the sky is blue, not brown !

Where the dewy green leaves glisten,
  In some cool, calm retreat,

I long once more to listen,
    Through the hush of the summer heat,
To the music of song-birds, blending
    With the murmurings of glad streams,
Through the quivering leaves ascending
    Like melody heard in dreams.

To climb the breezy mountains,
    To lie 'mongst the long-leaved ferns,
By the gush of gurgling fountains,
    My weary spirit yearns ;
And to roam o'er the flower-gemmed meadows,
    By the woods and sparkling rills,
When the twilight's purple shadows
    Steal over the violet hills.

In our home by the dreamy river,
    Where, mother, I long to be,
I never grew sad, oh ! never,
    But the days passed pleasantly.
From the city's din and bustle,
    Dear mother, then let us go,
Where the lush, green grasses rustle,
    And the golden kingcups blow.

—— o ——

A SPRING MORNING RAMBLE.

On past the doorways of the town asleep
    I trudge, with hasty step and spirit light ;
Above, around, a solemn hush and deep
    Is reigning, while the stars, that all the night

Over the sleeping world their watches bright
   Have kept, like diamonds darkling far away,
Wax paler and more pale, and fade from sight
   In the mild twilight of the new-born day.

The long streets silent and deserted are,
   An hour hence that with busy life will teem ;
Pale, weary toiling ones, from near and far,
   Wending their way—some as if in a dream—

To the close factories and the dusty mills,
   The livelong day to toil amidst the din
Of clattering looms and whirling iron wheels,
   Wearing their young lives out to keep them in.

But now I've reached that Garden of the Poor,[1]
   Where all alike may come and taste the sweets
Of Nature, here unfolded to allure
   The toil-worn from the city's crowded streets.

Here, n the summer, 'midst the buds and blooms,
   How sweet to breathe the pure, fresh, healthy air,
Rich with a thousand delicate perfumes,
   Stolen from a thousand flowers as sweetly fair !

Or, resting 'mongst the long, cool, pleasant grass,
   In the green shade of the low rustling trees,
To watch the white clouds through the blue sky pass,
   And listen to the song-birds' melodies.

Truly a noble gift, and one which round
   The donors' names hath cast a hallowed spell,
And in the people's hearts for them hath found
   A home, there, warmly cherished, aye to dwell.

[1] Baxter Park, Dundee.

As o'er the elastic dewy lawn I tread,
  The bracing morning air comes calm and cool ;
The hardy crocus nods its golden head,
  While bends the pearly snowdrop beautiful.

The violet and the daisy, too, I see,
  Recalling visions of the summer's prime ;
And cometh over hedgerow, plant, and tree,
  The greening glories of the sweet spring-time.

Mounting far up to heaven, a tiny lark
  Winnows with fluttering wing the cool blue air,
Piping its matin hymn ; I can but hark
  To the glad notes re-echoing everywhere.

Now on the breezy eminence I stand,
  And what a beauteous scene before me lies !
Sol, on his purple throne sublimely grand,
  From the blue North Sea billows seems to rise.

And on the yellow sands afar break wild
  Bright amber waves in showers of glistening spray ;
While, calm and lovely as a sleeping child,
  Or a great golden mirror, lies the Tay,

Glassing the pearly clouds and azure sky,
  And the green, glory-smitten Fifan hills,
And the great, stately ships that silent lie
  On its broad breast.   My soul with rapture fills !

But hark ! the loud clank of the factory bell
  Proclaims the weary toilings of the day
Will soon begin.   Bright sun, glad scenes, farewell !
  To the close, dusty mill I must away.

PATHETIC MUSINGS.

TO ONE IN ETERNITY.

THE mournful call that comes to all, and knoweth no
    denying,
  Afar from me hath summoned thee, my soul's dear idol,
    home.
Now pale and chill, and calm and still, and motionless
    thou'rt lying
  In darkness, 'midst the cold, red, wormy loam.

Like a sweet, modest flower in spring, the ambient air
    perfuming,
  Its dewy petals opening whitely to the summer sun,
Thou'rt blighted in the flush of thy sweet beauty's richest
    blooming,
  Ere thy life's summer hours had well begun.

Where now the golden, blissful dreams within my soul I
    cherished,
  Of long bright years of tranquil joy, dear love, when thou
    wert near?
All, all are faded from my life; all, all with thee have
    perished :
  I could not think to me thou wert so dear.

Thy soft, familiar voice no more I'll hear at early morning,
    Nor through the long, sad, weary day thine angel form
      will see ;
And never more at gloaming light, from the day's toil
    returning,
    Thy kindly smiles of love shall welcome me.

And, darling, I no more will twine thy pale-brown silken
    tresses,
    Nor clasp thee while I kiss thy rosy lips and snow-white
      brow ;
And thou no more wilt, smiling, chide my loving, fond
    caresses :
    Oh, can it be that I have lost thee now ?

Ah me ! the earth looks desolate ; my weary soul is darkling,
    Amidst a lonesome, dismal night of sorrow, deep and
      drear ;
On life's horizon, cold and bleak, no star at all is sparkling,
    The melancholy, mournful gloom to cheer.

The balmy spring may come again, and hope and joy
    impart,
    And gaily deck the barren wintry wold with vernal bloom ;
But, oh, it cannot cheer the chilly winter of my heart !
    Its leaves of love lie withered on thy tomb.

And yet I think not, darling, thou art lost to me for ever ;
    Something within me whispers that—oh, joy !—we'll
    meet again
In holier spheres, beyond the stars, in time no more to
    sever,
    Where's neither sighing, sorrow, grief, nor pain.

Down in thy narrow bed,
  Darling, thou'rt laid to rest ;
Cold and dark, 'midst the silent dead,
  The green turf on thy breast.

Sadly I sit by thy grave,
  While the stars pale watches keep,
And far away o'er the lone sea wave
  The calm, white moonbeams sleep ;

And all around is still,
  Save the night-wind's plaintive wail,
And the slumb'rous sound of the rushing rill,
  Down in the piny dale.

Thy spirit seemeth near,
  And thy love tones, soft and low,
Like music fall on memory's ear,
  As heard in the long ago,

When we roamed by the rippling brook,
  In the shadowy primrose dell,
To learn from the leaves of Nature's book
  The lessons we loved so well ;

And gather the fresh wild-flowers,
  The cowslip and blue harebell,
Or rest in the shade of the cool, green bowers,
  Our tales of love to tell.

The world looks cold and drear
  Since thou wert borne away,
Where life seemed, darling, when thou wert near,
  But a long sunshiny day.

I lived but alone for thee,
  My idol, my all, wert thou ;
A star to light me o'er life's dark sea,
  But the path is rayless now.

And yet I would not part
  With thoughts that cling to thee,
For the deepest love a living heart
  Could e'er bestow on me.

.   .   .   .

The summer sun hath sunk away, the amber daylight fades,
And over all in silence fall the gloaming's violet shades,
While dreamily and lone I wander by the moaning sea,
Sadly musing on thee, darling, lost on earth to me ;

And summoning old memories from out the misty past,
The dear old memories of joys too blissful long to last,
When thou wert by my side; and all the words and actions
    kind
Which thou hast said and done to me go flitting through
    my mind.

To think as 'twere but yesterday thou wert, in all thy pride
Of youth and health and loveliness, a joyous, blooming
    bride !
I felt so proud about thee while I clasped thee to my
    heart,
The thought had never passed my mind that we should
    ever part.

I feel so lone without thee now, while wand'ring on life's
    way,
E'en gloomy looks the golden sunlight of the summer
    day ;

The melody of song-birds, and the sweet wild-flowers that
    spring,
No joy or comfort to mine aching, weary heart can bring.

But oh, how changed when thou wert near in all thy
    youthful bloom !
Thy presence shed a halo bright around where all was
    gloom.
Now all day long I think about the face I cannot see ;
I wonder, love, where'er thou art, if thou dost think of me.

And often through the night, in dreams I wait again for
    thee
Beneath the shady green leaves of the hallowed trysting
    tree ;
We roam as we were wont, beside the glassy, gurgling rill,
Adown the glade and by the mossgrown ruins of the mill.

I cull the blue forget-me-not and wild rose blooming fair,
As I have done so oft, to gem thy pale-brown silken hair ;
Again thy love tones on mine ear all sweet and softly fall,
As far-off sounds of Sabbath bells the worshippers that
    call.

Oh, then I feel so glad, until I wake, and on my soul
The mournful truths come rushing, as wild, darksome
    billows roll
Upon a barren sea-shore, and I almost wish to be
Beside thee, darling, for I know thou'lt never come to me !

.   .   .   .

     Again night's sombre shadows flit
       In solemn stillness round,
     While tearfully and sad I sit
       Beside the grassy mound,

Where, in the quiet, dreamless rest,
　Dear love, thou'rt lying low,
And where, above thy silent breast,
　The summer flowers now blow.

The night-winds dirge-like moaning make
　Amongst the leaves and grass ;
Alas ! they cannot thee awake,
　Though o'er thy grave they pass.

A blackbird lone sits piping near,
　Upon the churchyard wall ;
Its mellow notes upon thine ear
　In mournful silence fall.

Oh, can it be, love, thou art hid,
　All lifeless, pale, and cold,
In darkness 'neath the coffin-lid,
　Low in the dank red mould ?

And will I see thy form divine
　No more, nor hear thee speak,
Nor press thy throbbing heart to mine,
　And kiss thy warm, soft cheek ?

I pause to listen, but in vain,
　Thou answerest not a word ;
Ah no ! thy soft, sweet voice again
　On earth will ne'er be heard.

Thy kindly heart is still, thine eye's
　Soft light no more will shine :
Yes, thou art dead, and joy has fled
　This weary heart of mine.

But though thy voice I cannot hear,
   Nor yet thy form can see,
I deem in spirit thou art near,
   In sympathy with me.

———o———

IN MEMORIAM :

AN OLD FRIEND.

AND is it so, old friend, that thou art hid
   For evermore away from mortal sight,
The grave-mould heaped upon thy coffin-lid,
   Thy sun of life eclipsed by death's dark night ?

Ah yes ! thy earthly mission is fulfilled,
   Life's cares and turmoil now for thee are o'er ;
The throbbing of thy genial heart is stilled,
   Thy kindly voice is mute for evermore.

A husband tender, true, and kind wert thou ;
   A parent loved and honoured and revered ;
A faithful friend, esteemed by all ; and now
   Thy memory to our hearts remains endeared.

The home thy presence rendered glad so long
   Seems dull and cheerless now, of thee bereft ;
Oh, thou art sorely missed and mourned among
   The sorrow-stricken loved ones thou hast left !

Idly to see thy well-known form they look
   Along the garden paths, where oft for hours
Thou'd pore upon the leaves of Nature's book,
   Tending with careful hand thy fav'rite flowers.

The little birds with liberal hand thou fed,
   Their old familiar songs for thee in vain
Will warble in the bare boughs overhead,
   While wondering that thou comest not again.

Vainly thy faithful dog shall watch and wait,
   With anxious, pleading look, and piteous moan,
To hear his master's footfall at the gate :
   He recks not thou art lying cold and lone.

O faithful friend ! O husband true and kind !
   O parent loved ! ' not dead but gone before ; '
Not long in grief shall we remain behind,
   When we must join thee on the unseen shore.

——o——

THE PICTURE ON THE WALL.

Down through a stirless atmosphere
   Falleth the dusky twilight gloom,
Shading mountain, vale, and mere,
   And stealing into my little room,

Where, by the firelight, flickering low,
   Dreamily, lone, and sad I sit,
Watching the red flames come and go,
   And their faintly glimmering shadows flit.

Silent and fitfully they pass
　　Over the room walls to and fro ;
Now they gleam on the looking-glass,
　　Now on the quaint old clock they glow.

Now on a pictured face they fall,
　　The fair young face of my dear, dead love,
Which looketh down on me from the wall,
ʿ　Like a beautiful angel from above.

Its large eyes, mildly blue and bright,
　　Its brown hair arching a noble brow,
And the full round cheeks all flushed and white--
　　It seemeth to smile upon me now,

Sweet as in life it used to smile ;
　　Yet it seemeth a living face to me,
For time that face can not erase
　　From the mirror of my memory.

It haunteth my vision all the day,
　　And floateth around me everywhere ;
And at night, when I look up far away
　　Among the stars, I see it there.

It rises before me in my dreams,
　　In the quiet hours of the mirk midnight,
And sometimes around it mildly gleams
　　A radiant halo of heavenly light.

And oft we roam where the limpid brook
　　Kisses the pebbles, white and cool,
And rest in the greenly-sheltered nook,
　　Close by the old mill's glassy pool ;

Rest 'neath the rustling tall old pine,
  Where oft we've met in the gloaming grey,
And I press her warm red lips to mine,
  And kiss her again in the dear old way.

Vain, idle dreams !   Ah, never again
  On earth that face will smile on me ;
It shineth where joys eternal reign,
  On the golden shore by the crystal sea.

And I am weary the livelong day,
  Lonely, restless, and sad at heart,
Longing to join her far away,
  Never more from my love to part.

———o———

RECALLED HOME.

SHE looked so lovely as she lay
  Within her snowy shroud,
While, like a far-shed sunset ray
  Tinging a pure white cloud,
A faint rose-colour flushed her cheek,
  A mystic radiance beamed
Around her face : in peaceful sleep
  Our little darling seemed.

Ah me ! as when at set of sun
  The purple clouds grow grey,
So paled the carmine flush that on
  Her waxen features lay.

Ah ! then we knew her spirit pure
    Had winged its flight through space,
Which but appeared to us before
    To linger round her face.

And oh, what anguish in that hour
    Our stricken hearts went through !
Our rosebud was the only flower
    Our wedding garden knew.
And oh, the gloom that shadowed all
    Our tear-dimmed vision met !
It seemed to us the gloaming fall
    Long ere the sun had set.

We bore her hence, to see her face
    No more, save but in dreams ;
And now a dull and empty place
    Our once bright dwelling seems.
Till sad and tenderly we laid
    Her 'neath the wild March flowers,
We had no thought her being made
    So much a part of ours.

A tiny lock of golden hair
    Fondly we linger o'er ;
And, sorrow blind, we call to mind
    The joys that are no more.
Our tears we struggle to repress,
    They all unconscious flow ;
With time, in place of lessening,
    Our sorrow seems to grow.

Yet wherefore grieve and murmur thus
    Against the high behest

Of Him who ruleth over us,
    And knoweth all things best ?
Ah ! if He had not deemed it wise
    His purpose to fulfil,
Our flower that blooms in Paradise
    Had graced our garden still.

———o———

THE FLOWER FADETH.

WE watched beside her dying couch
    So silently and sad,
As if our presence kept the chill
    Of death from all we had.

She looked serenely beautiful,
    Her face so pale and red,
As the angel spirit lingered
    'Twixt the living and the dead.

We knelt beside her little bed,
    And breathed a solemn prayer ;
A holy quiet fell around,
    Death's messenger was there.

At midnight's lonely, mystic hour,
    The dewy death-chill fell,
And ere the March light dawned, her soul
    Was where the angels dwell.

Rest, darling babe, our dear, dead rosebud, rest ;
  Thy little pilgrimage on earth is o'er,
Ere yet thy sun of infancy had ceased
  To shed refulgent glory on life's shore.

Rest, baby, though not weary, seek to rest ;
  Thy tiny limbs are rigid, pale, and chill ;
Thy rosy lips, which we so oft have pressed,
  Are cold ; thy voice and feet, ah me ! how still !

Rest, baby, rest in silence and in peace ;
  Soon shall thy lifeless form be hid from sight
In the still grave, where earthly sorrows cease,
  To sleep through one long, darkly silent night.

Vast empires, nations, all shall fade and die,
  Ages successive roll with endless sway ;
While thy immortal soul shall bloom on high,
  And soar through regions of eternal day.

—— o ——

THE FISHERMAN'S RETURN.

THE autumn sun hath sunk unseen,
All nature wears a sullen mien,
The face of heaven all grimly scowls,
And fierce and wild the loud wind howls
Around the fisherman's hut, which stands
In solitude by the brown sea sands.

In the doorway of that cottage rude
A woman stands in sorrowful mood,—
Stands in the gloom of the twilight bleak,
The salt tears glistening on her cheek,
Scanning with longing and anxious eye
The line where the ocean meets the sky.

And why does she gaze so wistfully
Over that dark, tumultuous sea?
And why do the tears roll down her cheek,
To hear the howl of the tempest bleak,
And the angry ocean's awful roar
Breaking white on the lone sea-shore?

Alas! far out on that billowy sea,
Where shriek the winds in their wildest glee,
'Midst the yawning breakers a tiny bark
Is madly tossed; through the storm and dark,
Brave hearts are striving in vain to reach
The lonely hut by the brown sea-beach.

Sadly around and over all
The dark hath come like a funeral pall;
Now in the hut by the dull hearthstone
The fisherman's young wife sits alone,
While fast from her eyelids the tear-drops start,
Upwelling deep from an aching heart.

Weary watching, she sinks to sleep,
Her thoughts far out on the stormy deep;
In dreams again by the bleak sea-beach
She stands, and, far as the eye can reach
Through the trailing mist-clouds, she descries
A speck on the waters fall and rise.

Her heart quick throbs 'twixt joy and fear,
As nearer it comes, and still more near,
Bounding swift as a wild sea-bird
Over the white foam madly stirred ;
Now through the murky gloom she can see
Dimly a form—'tis he ! 'tis he !

Hark to that cry through the rushing gale !
Where, oh ! where is the dark brown sail,
The brave, true hearts, and the tiny bark
That rode so well through the storm and dark ?
Buried, alas, by a treacherous wave,
Fathoms down in an ocean grave.

A corpse lies stark on the sandy shore,
Which mournfully she is bending o'er,
The picture of woeful, wild despair,
Tenderly stroking its tangled hair,
Pressing its lips, so pale and chill,
Clasping its fingers, so stiff and still.

She starts, she wakes from that dismal dream,
The sunbeams bright through the lattice stream :
The stormy winds are lulled to rest,
The waves lie still on the ocean's breast,
Mirroring skies serene and fair,
As if no storm had ever been there.

She stands again by the salt sea main,
Now with her young heart void of pain ;
At a little distance from the shore,
Calmly a boat comes sailing o'er
The toying wavelets, like liquid gold,
Last seen in the might of the tempest rolled.

D

Safely the boat hath come to land ;
The fisherman leaps on the sea-kissed sand,
He clasps her lovingly to his breast,
His lips to hers are fondly pressed,
While tears of joy rain down her face :
All grief is forgot in that dear embrace.

——o——

A FATHER'S LAMENT FOR HIS BAIRN.

OUR dear wee lammie's gane,
    She's sleepin' calm and soun'
Aneath the cauld gravestane,
    Whaur we hae laid her doon.
And oh, my heart is sair,
    To think that I will see
Her face on earth nae mair,
    That face sae dear to me !

I miss her nicht and morn,
    I miss her through the day ;
I'm lanely and forlorn,
    Alas, as weel I may.
I think on a' her wiles,
    Sae pawky and sae sly,
Her cheery voice and smiles ;
    And while I think, I sigh.

Ah yes ! I sadly sigh,
    To think nae mair she'll rin
To welcome me when I
    At meal hours do come in ;

Nor climb my elbow chair,
    Upon my knee to steal,
Alang wi' me to share
    The hamely, frugal meal.

I whiles forget, and look
    For her the house owre a',
For I can scarcely brook
    The thocht that she's awa' ;
The thocht that she lies still,
    Rowed in her wee white shroud,
The grave mould, damp and chill,
    Upon her locks o' gowd.

'Tis sinful to repine ;
    It was oor Father's will
That we oor bairn should tine,
    But oh, I tak' it ill !
Yet ae thocht cheers my soul,
    Like a lane star sae bricht,
Shinin' through clouds that roll
    Black owre the face o' nicht :

The thocht that though her form
    Lies cauld aneath the sod,
Food for the hungry worm,
    Her soul is safe wi' God,
Far on the shores o' bliss,
    'Mang angels pure and fair ;
And maybe, after this,
    We'll meet oor lammie there.

——o——

THE DYING WIFE TO HER HUSBAND.

OH, Sandy, press thy cheek to mine,
    But dinna grieve sae sair,
And kiss the lips thou sune wilt tine
    On earth for evermair ;
The lips sae aften prest to thine
In ecstacy o' joy divine,
Sin' we forgaithered lang, lang syne,
    Oor young hearts free o' care.

Oh, Sandy, can it be that noo
    Oor twa young hearts maun part ?
Oor wedded days hae been sae few,
    Sae dear to me thou art.
Alas ! it maun be sae ; the dew
O' death lies clammy on my broo,
My lips hae lost their rosy hue,
They're cauld and wan and moistless noo,
    A chill is owre my heart.

My een, whaur glinted ance the licht
    O' love, just like a star
That blinks sae bonnily and bright
    In the blue lift afar,
Grow dim, as stars 'mid cluds o' nicht,
Or violets nipt by an April blicht ;
For ever on my weary sicht
    Earth's glories faded are.

The wee birds, 'mang the dark green wuds,
    Noo sing in vain for me ;

The simmer's flush o' blooms and buds,
    That deck the grassy lee,
The blue hills and the siller cluds,
The sunset's gowden glory floods,
The glorious starry host that studs
    The heavens, nae mair I'll see.

My thochts gang back to lang past days,
    When we, twa gleesome bairns,
Sported whaur blythe the burnie plays
    Amang the rocks and ferns ;
And clamb the bloomy whin-clad braes,
Or roamed far in the tangled maze
O' rustlin' wuds, while birds sang lays,
    Lóve's alphabet to learn's.

But, love, oh dinna grieve sae sair !
    It only gies me pain ;
The heavy sorrow seek to bear
    Wi' strength no' a' thine ain.
Oor dear wee lammie lying there
A faither and a mither's care
Will claim frae thee, when I nae mair
    Can watch the helpless wean.

I'm laith, O love, to part frae thee,—
    But 'tis oor Faither's will,—
Thou'st been sae kind an' true to me
    While climbin' life's steep hill.
But thou wilt come sometimes and see
My grave, and kindly think o' me ;
Then, Sandy, fare thee weel ! till we
    Do meet in heaven, fareweel !

THE STORM.

AWAKE on her tear-wet pillow,
  The sailor's young wife lay,
Trembling to hear the great sea-billow
  Break on the beach of the bay ;

While her lonely heart with anguish throbbed
  For the loved one sailing afar,
As she heard the roar of the storm on shore,
  And the breakers on the bar.

She pressed her wee lamb to her breast,
  With a mother's tender care,
As she thought of the father far at sea,
  Whose image was mirrored there.

She kissed it o'er and o'er, with the love
  That only a mother knows ;
While the salt tears glistened on her cheek,
  Like dew on the pale primrose.

To the Father who ruleth over all,
  And rides on the surging foam,
She breathed a prayer that He might guard
  Her sailor safely home.

Still the storm-king shrieked in his fiendish glee,
  And madly swept along,
While the throb of that young heart rose and fell
  To the notes of his wild death-song.

The morning dawned, and the tempest wild
    Had sung itself to sleep,
And the crested billows were rocked to rest
    O'er the face of the gloomy deep.

And sadly she stood by the bleak sea-beach,
    And gazed o'er the mournful main ;
But her brown-haired, blue-eyed sailor lad
    Came never back again.

He lies in a shroud of the green seaweed,
    By the wild Norwegian steep ;
And vainly for him by the desolate shore
    The widow may watch and weep.

———*o*———

THE SUICIDE.

    THE silent moon
Reigns queen of heaven, with silvery splendour crowned,
    Dispelling midnight gloom,
Shedding pale rays of holy light around ;
  Far off, in mournful peals, the city bell
  Chimes forth the mystic hour, a solemn knell.

    In yonder vale,
By the dark rolling river's rocky brink,
    Wanders a maiden pale ;
Thoughts fill her soul, alas, from which we shrink :
  That sad young heart o'erflows with silent grief,
  In this dark vale of tears her hours are brief.

Love's earliest dream,
Holy and pure, within her breast had burned ;
But like the flowing stream
That feeds the hungry deep, 'twas unreturned :
In vain that hopeless love she sought to quell,—
A broken heart is hers, she loved too well.

To breathe a prayer
She bends the knee ; dread silence reigns around :
Traces of dark despair
And anguish deep in that pale face are found ;
Love's sunshine gleams no more, hope to impart,
Soothing that poor forlorn, forsaken heart.

Hark ! a dull splash :
'Tis past, and all is silent as before ;
'Twas but the wavelet's dash
Against the frowning cliffs on either shore ;
But, hush ! a low, faint moan steals through the air :
The chill waves close around that maiden fair.

The angels' tears
In dewdrops gently fall upon the sod ;
A soul, young in its years,
Is struggling 'twixt her bosom and its God
In vain ; the deep, dark river rolls o'erhead :
Her spirit soars, she's numbered with the dead.

——o——

PARTING WORDS.

Mother, my wasted limbs wax numb and chill,
   The icy hand of death is on me now ;
The throbbings of my weary heart grow still,
   And beads of clammy sweat stand on my brow.

Open the casement, mother ; let me gaze
   Once more upon the landscape green and fair.
Mother, come near me and my pillow raise ;
   Ah, now how cool and sweet the summer air !

Upon our garden tree the linnet trills
   To me its farewell song, and now mine eyes,
For the last time, behold the glancing rills,
   And the green far-off hills that grandly rise.

Their smiling peaks, with sunrise glory clad,
   Point to a holier home, far, far away,
And I will soon be there ; but oh, how sad
   To think I leave thee here alone to stay !

No earthly friend to love thee, none to cheer
   Thy lonely heart, when I am lowly laid
In the cold graveyard.   Oh, my mother dear,
   Still trust in Him whose love can never fade !

Lay me down softly, mother.   Now I feel
   The chilly hand of death press on my breast ;
But glorious visions on my fancy steal,
   And angels bright are kissing me to rest.

THE SISTER'S DREAM.

I'M very sad and lonely, mother,
  Watching day by day ;
Oh, tell me why my darling brother
  Stays so long away ?

The summer's fled, the flowers gay
  Have died on hill and plain,
And not a garland woven ; say,
  When will he come again ?

I've waited, watched, and wearied through
  The cold, dark, wintry hours ;
By brook and glade alone I've strayed,
  To cull the wild spring flowers.

I've chased the bee o'er hill and lea,
  When summer days were long,
And in the golden harvest fields
  I've heard the reapers' song.

Yet still he comes not: oh, how drear
  And sad the long hours seem !
But I will tell thee, mother dear,
  A strange but lovely dream.

To-day, beside the reedy rill
  Down in the dusky dell,
I ran about till wearied out,
  At last asleep I fell.

And then methought from heaven came down
  An angel all in white,
Upon its head a golden crown,
  Magnificently bright.

The angel smiled and beckoned me,
  And far away we flew,
By silvery clouds, amidst a sea
  Of calm and shining blue,

Until we reached a distant star,
  So wondrous large and bright,
Though small and pale it looked afar ;
  And what a glorious sight

My vision met ! for there I saw,
  In shining raiment clad,
My brother dear.   But then, mamma,
  I woke, alone and sad.

Calm thy young sorrows, darling sweet,
  Thy brother's all are o'er ;
Pray God to guide thee, and thou'lt meet
  Him on that heavenly shore ;

And white-winged seraphs' songs will give
  Thee joyful welcoming,
Where flowers of love immortal live
  Through one eternal spring.

———0———

THE BLIGHTED FLOWER.

LEFT to wander in the sinful city,
  Helpless and forlorn,
Not a friend my wretched fate to pity,
  Subject to the scorn
And insult of night-prowlers passing by,
Who mock my misery. Ah me ! but I
Could gladly lay me down, unseen, to die,
  With my wee babe unborn.

In fitful gusts the piercing wintry blast
  Howls down the narrow street,
The blinding raindrops heavily and fast
  On pane and pavement beat ;
But from the chill breath of the cruel wind,
Which blows the rain about me so unkind,
Alas, alas ! no shelter can I find :
  Would death come now, 'twere sweet.

Afar I see the lights gleam, where the river
  Is rolling dark and wide ;
I'll go and drown my hopeless woes for ever
  Beneath its stormy tide.
What do I say ? God help me in this hour
Of trial ! shield me from the tempter's power ;
Dispel the rayless glooms that o'er me lower,
  And my weak footsteps guide !

I have a home—'tis far away from here—
  Where dear ones mourn for me

As being worse than dead.   I long, but fear,
    Them all again to see ;
To lay my head on mother's bosom, if
But only to entreat her to forgive
Her erring child, worthy no more to live
    Under the old roof-tree.

I was so happy in the peaceful glen,
    Before the tempter came
To wile me from the dear old home, till then
    Of pure and stainless fame.
My mother, good and kind, why did I grieve her?
The dearest friend of all, why did I leave her,
To follow one—a heartless, base deceiver—
    To misery and shame?

But I'll go back, though long the way and dreary,
    Though mirk the night and chill ;
Through wind and rain, though weak my limbs and
        weary :
    With God's help, yes, I will !
I go, I go !   Even now, my mother dear,
Methinks thy old familiar voice I hear,
· Striving with kindly words to soothe and cheer
That sinful, broken heart, which soon, I fear,
    Will moulder cold and still.

———o———

LINES TO A SORROWING ONE.

AND thou art well-nigh left alone,
  In this cold world of care and strife ;
Dark, wintry shadows have been thrown
  Athwart the summer of thy life.

Thy pure young heart, which should have known
  But blissful dreams and joyous hours,
Is sad ; thy pathway hath been strewn
  With thorns, where should have bloomed but flowers.

The sun of joy but dim hath shone
  Around thee, e'en from childhood's years ;
Thy nearest, dearest friends have gone,
  And left thee lonely in thy tears.

A father's love thy soul hath yearned
  In vain to know or feel ; death came
For him ere yet thy lips had learned
  To lisp aright the hallowed name.

And now a mother's tender care
  Thy sorrowing heart no more can know ;
No brother near thee now to share
  Thy grief, or soothe thee in thy woe.

Keep heart, dear sister, ne'er despair ;
  The sun shines brightest after rain,
The thunderstorm makes pure the air,
  And joy is sweetest after pain.

Though bleak to thee the world now seems,
  Though dark thy night of sorrow lowers,
Hope's star will rise ; its mild, glad beams
  Shall wake to life thy heart's joy-flowers,

To bloom, God grant, through long bright years,
  With one more dear than all to thee,—
One who will kiss away thy tears,
  And cheer thee sailing o'er life's sea.

———o———

LILY RAY.

CLOSE beside a glassy brook,
  Murmuring on with many a wimple,
Sheltered in a cool green nook,
  Stood a cottage plain and simple,
Now, alas, gone to decay,—
'Twas the home of Lily Ray.

There she lived, her parents' pride ;
  Death of many had bereft them,
All had faded from their side,
  Lily only God had left them ;
But a sweeter flower, I ween,
Or a purer, ne'er was seen.

She was gentle, she was fair,
  With her blue eyes mildly beaming
Full of love, her golden hair
  Down her milk-white shoulders streaming

In long, graceful, wavy curls,
And her teeth twin rows of pearls.

And her cheeks were like the dawn
   Of a lovely summer morning ;
As she tripped by dale or lawn,
   Scarce she touched the flowers adorning
The greensward, while all the way
Sunshine followed Lily Ray.

Ah me ! but my heart grows sad,
   As on youthful days I ponder,
When, with footsteps free and glad,
   'Midst the green wilds we would wander,
Happy all the summer day,
Me and blue-eyed Lily Ray.

Then our hearts no sorrow knew,
   Pleasant dreams the day passed o'er us,
All things looked so fair to view ;
   And we fancied life before us
Lay bright, boundless, calm, and free,
As the broad blue summer sea.

Childhood's golden hours passed by,
   Fate decreed that we should sever,
And we vowed with many a sigh
   To forget each other never ;
Then I thought our hearts had broken,
When the last farewell was spoken.

Summer went, and winter hoar
   Came with breath so dank and chilly ;

But I saw her never more—
   Golden-haired, bright, blue-eyed Lily ;
She had joined the spirit band,
In the viewless, mystic land.

Many summers since have fled,
   Still I think of Lily only,
Darkling in her narrow bed,
   And my life seems very lonely ;
But at midnight, still and drear,
Oft in dreams her voice I hear.

———o———

WATCHING IN VAIN.

A MAIDEN sat lone on a mossy stone,
   Close by the moaning midnight sea,
Singing with sad and plaintive tone,
' I am weary watching here alone,
   Oh, come back, love, to me !'
But the night-winds cried with a hollow groan,
And the sea replied with a sullen moan,
   ' He will never come back to thee !'

Her face gleamed white in the weird moonlight,
   That silvered the surging, blue, lone sea,
As she looked away, far out in the bay,
O'er the foam-capped waves, through the misty spray
   By the wind blown far and free,
Singing with sad and plaintive tone,
' I am weary watching here alone,
   Oh, come back, love, to me !'

E

While the night-winds cried with a hollow groan,
And the waves replied with a sullen moan,
  ' He will never come back to thee !'

No tear stood on her white, white cheek,
  Nor shone in her bright but hollow eye ;
Ah, no ! the fountains of the heart,
That open with sorrow's bitter smart,
And flow to the eyes, and in teardrops start,
  Had long in her been dry,
As to and fro she swayed and sang,
While mournfully the echoes rang,
  Borne through the midnight sky,

' I am weary watching here alone ;
  Oh, cruel, cruel sea,
Have pity, and send back my own
  True-hearted love to me !
For he has vowed, when he comes home,
  That I his bride will be.'
But the winds still cried with a hollow groan,
And the waves replied with a sullen moan,
  ' He will never come back to thee !'

Oh, long she sat, but she looked in vain
  Over the misty moonlit tide
For him who would never return again,
  To make her his own dear bride !
For soundly he slept in the deep, far down,
Wrapt in a shroud of the seaweed brown,
And never more in the seaport town
  Would he sit by her side.

Yet oft she sits on the mossy stone,
  Gazing sadly over the sea ;
And still she sings in a hopeless tone,
' I am weary, weary watching alone,
  Will you never come back to me ? '
But still the groaning night-winds cry,
And still the moaning waves reply,
  ' He will never come back to thee ! '

—————o—————

MEMORIES OF CHILDHOOD.

SNUGLY sheltered by a shady wild wood,
  In the hollow of a steep green hill,
Stands a cot, the dear home of my childhood,
  Close beside a babbling mountain rill.

Oh, what joyous days and cheerful gloamings
  Were mine beside that cot, now far away !
And there was one, my mate in all my roamings,
  Golden-hair'd, bright, blue-eyed Lily Ray.

When chill dark hoary winter field and mountain
  Had clad with snowy raiment, and had bound
With icy chains each brooklet, pool, and fountain,
  And all lay bare and desolate around,

Unmindful of the storm, we'd march each morning,
  With merry hearts, a mile or more to school,
And linger oftentimes at dusk returning,
  To slide upon the marshy frozen pool.

And when spring came, her balmy breathings breaking
    The icy fetters forged by winter's cold,
Sending the rills forth singing, and awaking
    To verdant bloomy life the barren wold,

With gladdened sight we saw the flowers upspringing,
    And the green buds from plant and hedgerow peer ;
With raptured ear we heard again the singing
    Of Nature's choir,—songs to our hearts so dear.

And when sweet-smiling summer had unfolden
    Her emerald banners over vale and hill,
Spangled with floral gems, pale-blue and golden,
    The daisy, speedwell, spink, and daffodil,

Through dusky dell and woodland gaily straying,
    Around her silken hair the flowers I'd twine ;
Whilst singing birds, and brooks, and soft winds playing
    Among the leaves, made melody divine.

And when the autumn sun shone mild and mellow
    O'er holm and height, thick set with golden sheaves;
When juicy peach and apple glistened yellow
    On garden wall and tree, 'midst browning leaves,—

All through the glad vacation-time we'd ramble
    O'er the wild moors, and through the songless wood,
And pluck the scarlet hypp, the nut, and bramble,
    In tangled brake and rocky solitude.·

And now the treasured, hallowed recollections,
    And sunny memories of childhood's years,
Waken my heart's best feelings and affections,
    And I look dimly through a mist of tears.

Miscellaneous Rhymes.

MISCELLANEOUS RHYMES.

———◆———

A DREAM OF THE FUTURE.

WITH prophet-eyes I scan the future dim ; there roll away
The mists of error in the glorious dawn of reason's day ;
The 'sun of peace' arises, never more its light to wane,—
A golden halo shedding over every land and main.

No more the direful war-cry wildly rings beneath the
    skies;
The bloody sword is sheathed, in strife no more it shall
    arise ;
The holy balm of love, like fragrance from a trampled flower,
From human hearts arises, making earth an Eden bower.

The slave's deep wail is hushed ; now, like the 'ransomed
    ones ' above,
Their chains are bonds of universal brotherhood and love ;
The world's great heart is melted by that truth, whose
    light sublime
Alone the grain can golden for that happy harvest-time,
When peace and love o'er all the earth immortally shall
    bloom,
And paradise is opened up on either side the tomb.

STRIVE TO LOVE EACH OTHER.

STRIVE to love each other,
    Heart and soul sincere ;
Court each as a brother,
    Or a sister dear.
Few our days, and weary,
    Full of hopes and fears ;
Dark the road and dreary
    Through this vale of tears.

Sadly and complaining,
    Trudge we on through life ;
Where peace might be reigning,
    There is nought but strife.
Love from hearts upwelling
    Might fill all the earth,
Light each lordly dwelling,
    Cheer each lowly hearth.

Help ye one another,
    Idly scorn to live ;
To a forlorn brother
    Hopeful counsel give ;
Kind words mildly spoken
    Leave no bitter smart,
They soothe the spirit broken,
    Heal the wounded heart.

Human hearts beat kindly,
    Full of love untold;

But men, groping blindly
    Ever after gold,
Coldly spurn each other,
    Passing on life's road—
Offspring from one mother,
    One great Father, GOD.

———o———

SCOTIA'S WELCOME TO THE PRINCESS
ALEXANDRA.

FROM thy home over the sea,
Daughter of Denmark, thou comest, the idol of all ;
    Scotia with one heart greets thee,
Ten thousand welcomes await thee from cottage and hall.
        Ring the bells merrily,
            Greet her with hearts full of glee ;
        Welcome her cheerily
            From her home over the sea.

Thou comest with beautiful spring,
Pure as the daisy that gems her bright garment of green ;
    Meet bride for the future king
Of the mightiest nation and empire the world has seen.
        High let the banners wave,
            Peacefully, proudly, and free ;
        Greet her triumphantly
            From her home over the sea.

From the lonely isles of the west,
To the busy, fertile shores of the German Sea,

Let all from their labours rest,
Let all rejoice in the day of jubilee.
Let mirth and song abound,
Sighing and sorrow all flee ;
Let drum and trumpets' sound
Greet her from over the sea.

Brave sons of the Celt, arise !
Let the bonfire blaze on the grand old hills of Braemar ;
Shout till your joyous cries
Awaken the echoes that slumber on dark Lochnagar ;
Let the shrill pibroch ring
Far up the glens of the Dee ;
Welcome your future king's
Bride from her home o'er the sea.

Oh, may the bright star of love
Linger around thee, and joy find a home in thy heart !
May the great Father above
His choicest blessing to thy happy union impart !
This be our earnest prayer,
Solemnly bending the knee :
God guide the loving pair
Safe o'er life's perilous sea !

———o———

LINES ON THE ROYAL VISIT TO DUNDEE.

THEY come from their home 'midst the Highland hills
Of purple heather, where sparkling rills
Ripplingly wander o'er ferny fells,

And dash down the depths of lone, shadowy dells
In foaming cascades of starry spray,
And the wild deer merrily bounds away.

They come, and with joy and pride, to-day
   Ten times ten thousand loyal hearts
Are throbbing, all waiting their homage to pay,—
   A love which the soul, not the voice, imparts.

Flags and banners are flaunting and streaming
   Gaily, far up in the autumn air ;
Streets and windows and housetops are teeming
With myriad forms, their faces all beaming
   With gladness, to welcome the royal pair.

     But hark to the trumpet's blare,
       And the soul-stirring roll of the drum !
     Now fitfully through the air
       Arises a mighty hum
     Of multitudinous voices ;
     The expectant crowd rejoices
To hear the welcome cry, 'They come, they come !'

     And the long, dense lines of human life
       Press eagerly to and fro,
    To catch a glimpse, in the joyous strife,
    Of their future king and his fair young wife,
      Who in triumph onward go.

From balcony and casement, ladies bright
   Enthusiastically look down, and wave
With lily hands their kerchiefs snowy white ;
   And cheers, that only greet the good and brave,

From the great surging multitude ascend.
  As the loud echoes of an Alpine pass
Resound from cliff to cliff when thunders rend
The clouds, so fly the cheers from end to end
Of the long living lines.   Their echoes blend
  With strains of martial music, till the mass
Delirious seems with gladness ; and from tower
  And steeple high, melodious-sounding bells
Ring out a merry, joyous peal to our
Beloved prince and princess, the sweet flower
  Of Denmark, who in all our hearts now dwells.

Out on the Tay's broad, bright-blue breast,
Ride at their anchors, in colours drest,
  Three vessels, with crews all brave,
Ready to bear o'er the North Sea foam
Our bonnie sweet bird to her dear old home.
  God speed her o'er the wave,
And guide her in safety back again
To her island home from the land of the Dane—
  The land she must always love !
On the loving pair, and the sweet wee flower
Which has grown from their marriage garden, shower
  Thy bounty from heaven above !

———o———

MY NEW HAME.

NEAR whaur the coaly Tyne weds wi' the sea,
In a canty wee hoose dwelt my wifie and me,
As cosy and snug as twa birds in a nest ;
But noo we hae flitted awa' to the west.

Awa' to the west, 'mang the Cumberland fells,
Whaur caller the wind blaws, and sweetly it smells,
And smokeless the sunlicht fu' bonnily gleams
On blue mountain tarns and clear rushing streams.

Oh, here in its beauty and freshness I see
Dame Nature's sweet face smilin' saftly on me !
In green, fertile valleys, besprinkled wi' trees,
That murmur and wave in the health-laden breeze,

And tall piny woods, wi' their dark, wavin' plumes ;
While shadow in silence and solitude glooms
In cool mossy nooks, deep in green sylvan dells ;
While far abune a' tower the dark, heathy fells.

On Eden's fair banks, i' the still gloamin' fa',
I pensively saunter, and fondly reca'
The memories dear o' the joys that langsyne
I shared wi' auld freends on the banks o' the Tyne.

How often I gaze ower the valley sae wide
To the bonnie green hills o' my ain countryside !
Even then, though my bosom wi' fond rapture thrills,
I sigh for a glimpse o' the Tyne ballast hills.

Yet still in sweet dreams, in the hush o' the nicht,
The scenes so familiar arise on my sicht ;
Then gaily I wander aince mair by the mill,
Up through the green valley to fair Primrose Hill.

For though here I'm contented, and neebors are kind,
I ever will cherish the freends left behind ;
And wherever I roam, or whate'er may betide,
My heart will aye warm to the canny Tyneside.

LINES TO MY ABSENT WIFE.

SERENELY calm the summer moon is shining
   Over the tranquil bosom of the Tay,
While lonely by the window I'm reclining,
   Thinking of you, dear Janet, far away.

With wistful, longing eyes I gaze far over
   The dusky woods and grey green hills of Fife ;
And long I strive, though vainly, to discover
   The well-known hill near where you are, dear wife.

That hallowed hill which we, in days of wooing,
   Have climbed with lightsome steps and hearts all glee,
Where the birds warbling, or the cushats cooing,
   Were not more glad or free from care than we.

Though far away, my thoughts are ever winging
   Their silent flight to the dear, red-roofed cot,
Round which so many memories are clinging
   Of sunny hours that ne'er can be forgot.

And oft with fancy's eye I see you sitting
   With kind old mother on the sunny green,
Sewing so busily, or deftly knitting,
   While o'er the soft grass scrambles ' baby Teen.'

The dear wee prattling cherub, how I miss her,
   With her old-fashioned ways, and ringing laughter,
And shrill ' ta-ta's ' !   For me be sure and kiss her
   A thousand times.   I will repay you after.

The holidays are nigh, and, oh, what gladness
  To be relieved from my appointed duties,
And leave the smoky town, its sin and sadness,
  To rusticate with Nature and her beauties !

I'm doubly joyful in anticipation
  Of the short respite from my toil ; for then,
As well as taste the sweets of recreation,
  I'll see dear baby's face and yours again.

———*o*———

TO MY ABSENT WIFE.

OH, Janet love, while standing on the pier
  When you and dear wee baby sailed away
Across the Tay's blue waters, glancing clear,
  So sad I felt though seeming to be gay.

But drearer grew my heart when home I went,
  With no one there to greet me with a smile ;
The house was dark and still, the fire was spent,
  And all looked dismal as a wintry isle.

I sought my couch ; mine eyelids would not close
  For thinking of our pet and you, dear wife ;
And when, all tired, I sank into repose,
  In dreams I was beside you, far in Fife,—

Beside you in the dear old rustic cot,
  Where now you are with mother kind and good ;
And loneliness and sadness were forgot,
  While round the fire we sat in merry mood.

The vision vanished,—you were far away ;
   I thought, ' Will she have also dreamt of me ? '
And not in dreams alone, but through the day,
   In fancy you and ' baby Teen ' I see.

Oh, to be with you from the dinsome town !
   I feel so jaded with its foul, close air ;
To climb Benarty, 'mongst the heather brown,
   The cool winds blowing round me everywhere ;

And wander by the Lochty and the Orr,
   Under the shady elms and beeches old ;
Or scale the mossy crags, so steep and hoar,
   That, next to you, I long so to behold.

How oft I think upon those hours so sweet,
   Whilst lovers, roaming 'midst these scenes so dear
Ah, then how bright earth seemed, and I'd repeat
   My simple rhymes you loved so well to hear.

And now we sail together on life's tide,
   And sunny days we've had, and cloudy too ;
But always, dear, since you became my bride,
   To me you've been so tender, kind, and true.

A kiss I waft to ' baby Teen ' and you ;
   And while you're gone may sunshine still prevail,
And the fresh air your wasted strength renew,
   And bring the rose back to your cheek so pale !

————0————

CHILDREN AT PLAY.

DOWN the far west, with gorgeous colours glowing,
    Sinks the red sun, all splendid and serene ;
The dreamy river, seaward calmly flowing,
    Is gilded over with an amber sheen.

In green and golden lines the fields lie smiling,
    All lustrous gleam the brown hills far away ;
While dreamily, an idle hour beguiling,
    I watch a group of little children play.

Down in the hollow of a mossy meadow,
    Where stands a solitary tall elm tree,
There, underneath its friendly, cool green shadow,
    Gambol and romp the younglings, full of glee.

Circling its trunk, huge, ivy-grown, and hoary,
    Hand joined in hand all merrily round they go ;
Wee golden heads glint in the sunset glory,
    Kissed by the wide-spread branches bending low.

The music of their clear, sweet voices, ringing
    Through the calm evening hush, to me appears
An old familiar melody, back bringing
    Dear memories of childhood's happy years.

And like a dream, a musing deep comes o'er me,
    Back a long lapse of years my fancies roam,
To youth's flower-budding season, when before me
    The world lay bright as heaven's cerulean dome.

Long-slumbering thoughts within my soul are wakened ;
　　Long-vanished hallowed scenes and forms, whose places
Long in the dear home circle have been vacant,
　　Through the dim, misty past my mind's eye traces.

Then, oh, rejoice, be glad, ye little children,
　　While the calm morning of your lives doth last !
For soon will come the day, with cares bewild'ring,
　　When ye shall sigh o'er childhood's pleasures past.

———ᴏ———

A STORY OF THE SEA.

MIRK and dense the clouds are lowering,
O'er the wild white billows towering
Mountains high, the salt spray showering
　　O'er the beetling cliffs ashore ;
Lurid gleams the sheeted lightning,
Night's bleak face all weirdly bright'ning,
But the storm-tost sailors whitening ;
　　Thunders peal, and chill winds roar.

'Midst that elemental crashing,
O'er that dark sea madly dashing,
Fiercely foaming, loudly lashing,
　　Landward drifts a fated barque.
Hark ! the booming guns are blending
With the thunder, heaven rending ;
See ! the blue lights far ascending,
　　Streaming meteors through the dark.

Denser grows the mist, and dimmer
Glows the fitful, lurid shimmer
Where the stern and toplights glimmer,
  Rocking wildly through the gloom.
Like a maddened war-horse rearing,
Leaping, plunging, swift careering,
Still the rugged low reef nearing,
  Rolls she onward to her doom.

Fiercer howls the blast, and louder
Burst the thunder-clouds that shroud her ;
Hark ! from trembling forms that crowd her
  Wave-washed decks wild shrieks arise :
Wailing screams of frantic women,
Mingling with hoarse cries of seamen,
Ringing, 'bove the tempest demon's
  Death-song, through the murky skies.

To destruction swift and swifter
On the rolling surges drift her ;
Now far up they lightly lift her,
  Now she's well-nigh lost to sight,—
Like a mighty sea-bird wheeling,
Like a drunken giant reeling ;
Gleams a lightning flash, revealing
  All around the breakers white.

Now the shore with life is teeming,
Flashing torch-lights red are gleaming,
Surging back the gloom, and streaming
  O'er that black, tumultuous sea
To the doomed ship, and seeming
Rays of hope through death's night beaming
To those souls, all wildly dreaming
  Of a dim eternity.

By that sea-beach, lashed so fearful,
Anxious women stand all tearful,
While brave hearts, all toiling cheerful,
   Drag the lifeboat to the strand.
Blinding spray-clouds each big wave throws
Shoreward ; fearlessly they brave those,
Ready death to meet, or save those
   Perishing so near to land.

Nobly calm they take their places
In the boat, of fear no traces
In those manly, rough brown faces,
   While amidst the surge they launch.
Now the low, dark reef they're rounding,
O'er the great white billows bounding,
Each against the black rocks sounding
   Like an Alpine avalanche.

Through the gloom wet eyes are straining,
While to sight the boat is waning,
Fast the fated vessel gaining ;
   Now her dancing light is seen
By the wreck ;—great Father, guide her !
For a space no harm betide her !—
Now the distance wide and wider
   Grows the wreck and boat between.

Safely from that foam-lashed, stranded
Vessel all on shore are landed ;
And to Him who erst commanded
   Galilee's wave to be still,
Many a humble knee low bendeth,
Many an earnest prayer ascendeth :
Thus, dear friends, my story endeth,
   Aid its purpose to fulfil.

FACE AT THE NURSERY WINDOW.

AWAY where the big town mingles
  With fields and garden lands,
Near to the dusty roadway,
  A neat wee cottage stands.

And in that neat wee cottage
  Once dwelt a maiden fair,
With rounded cheeks, rose-tinted,
  And long dark glossy hair.

And lips like the sweet geranium,
  And hazel-brown bright eyes,
And so comely, you'd have thought her
  An angel in disguise.

I passed this cottage daily,
  And I oftentimes would see
Her sitting beside the window
  Of the little nursery,

With a group of dear wee children
  All playing round her knee ;
And this pretty brown-eyed maiden
  Would sweetly smile to me.

Her loving smile brought sunshine
  To my lonely, weary heart,
And banished awhile the sorrows
  That form of life a part.

I felt quite melancholy,
 When passing up or down,
If I did not see at the window
 Those eyes of hazel-brown.

I grew to love that maiden,
 Yes, more than tongue can tell ;
And I thought by her smiles and blushes
 That she loved me as well.

But time, alas, brings changes :
 One day I missed her face,
And there sat by the nursery window
 Another in her place.

It seemed as if a shadow
 All darkly round me fell ;
A shadow which the sunshine,
 Alas ! could not dispel.

And still it hovers round me
 The weary night and day,
And only the light of her presence
 Can chase the gloom away.

Now up and down I wander,
 But I look in vain to see
The dear, familiar, sweet face
 That used to smile on me.

Yet I often look to the window,
 Though the face I may not find,
For it mirrors back the image
 That's fixed upon my mind.

LINES TO A LADY ON HER WEDDING MORN.

So thou art going, a joyous bride,
　　To share a home with one that's dear
To thy young heart ; God bless and guide
　　Thee in thy new and holy sphere !

Thine eyes be never dimmed with tears
　　Of sorrow, cares ne'er cloud thy brow,
But may thy love in after-years
　　Be shining, pure, and bright as now.

From out thy wedding garden may
　　A branch of love's sweet rosebuds spring ;
To blossom only to decay
　　With age, their offspring round thee cling.

And when thy voyage of life is o'er,
　　When thou must quit thine earthly home,
God bring thee to that sinless shore
　　Where earthly sorrows never come !

THE SONG OF HORAND.

THE wassail was drunk in the red wine old,
When Horand called for his harp of gold ;
His fingers over the strings he swept,
Awakening tones that for years had slept.

And bowl and beaker aside were pushed,
And jest and talk and laugh were hushed,
And the hall grew still as a night of snow,
And men and women their heads bent low,
While he sang, in a voice so soft and sad,
Of the ' Death of the Flowers,' a song he had
Made while he yet was a beardless lad,
Which pleased the maidens beyond all measure,
So that they wept for very pleasure.

Anon he upraised his voice in glee,
And warbled the old ' Lay of Amillee ; '
And so sweetly delightful was the strain,
That the old who listened felt young again,
And seemed to smell the fragrant flowers,
And hear the song-birds in the bowers ;
While the gladness of days forgotten long
Swelled up in their hearts with the minstrel's song.

For it told of all pleasant and lovely things,—
Of the bright days of summer, when verdure springs,
And sunshine lies on the purple hills,
And goldenly gleams on the laughing rills ;
And flowers all the desert heath perfume,
And roses at Campatilla bloom ;
When swallows to far north climes are called,
And nightingales sing in the Westerwald.

It told of shallops, with sails snow-white,
Faring on waters than heaven more bright ;
And of love that with old age ne'er decays,
And the sharp, sweet sorrows of wooing days.
It told of the joys of the perilous chase,
In the mellow glory of autumn days,

When the yellow leaves fall crisp and sere,
And the woods resound with the gladsome cheer,
And the merry notes of the bugle-horn
Through all the hours from early morn.

But suddenly his voice grew bold,
While he sang of the feuds and fights of old ;
Of the desperate conflicts, hand to hand,
On the desolate shores of the Wulpensand ;
Of the battles at Waleis and Balyan,—
Till the stern, brave warrior knights began
To clench their fists and knit their brows,
While the lion within their hearts would rouse.

Then he sang of the sea, how again and again
They had fought 'gainst the angry northern main,
And had borne the brunt of the tempest's might
Through many a long, dark, starless night ;
And had 'scaped the whirling maelstrom, tossed
By the wild and rugged Norwegian coast ;
And had seen the sun, at the night's pale noon,
O'er Thule's cliffs, red as the rising moon.

Then bating his voice, in a mournful strain
He sang of the brave and the noble slain,
Who had died in defence of the fatherland,
And peacefully slept on the Wulpensand.

But his voice grew softer, and sweeter his song,
While he told how fair times pass along,
And beauty and pleasure with them fly ;
How winter snow in the hair doth lie,
When the last still haven draweth nigh.

Then he sang of scenes and joys sublime
And holy, beyond the grave and time,
Till teardrops glistened on each fair cheek,
And the stern, brave hearts of the men grew weak.
But they were not sad, good sooth, not they,
   While listening to Horand's tender song ;
They were as glad as if far away
   On the heavenly shore with the angel throng.

When Horand ended his song, he bade
His page take the harp upon which he had played,
And cast it into the North Sea main,
For never more would he sing again.

———o———

THE DON VALLEY CALAMITY.[1]

THE stars are dimly peeping
Through the murky clouds, and keeping
Fitful watches o'er the weeping,
Weary world, to slumber gone.
   The March winds wild are sweeping,
   And the torrents loud are leaping
Down the hills, along the valley of the Don.

In the hamlets of the valley,
Heavy eyelids now are closing,
Weary forms are now reposing
From life's sorrows, sad and drear.

[1] Some years ago a large reservoir near Sheffield burst its embankment, when 250 persons were swept off with the flood.

They are lying, calmly dreaming,
Hushed in slumber, safe all seeming ;
But, ah me ! how little deeming
That the wrecker Death's so near.

On the night, still growing drearer,
Breaks a sound,—'tis coming nearer,
Waxing deeper, louder, clearer—
God of mercy, save us all !
With a roar like loudest thunder,
Bursting bridge and bank asunder,
Down the valley rolls the great white foaming wall.

Like a mighty tempest rushing
Through a wood, the great oaks crushing,
Wildly whirling, madly gushing,
On the awful deluge rolls.
Far and wide its seething waters
Death and desolation scatters,—
Fathers, mothers, sons and daughters ;—
Christ have mercy ! save their souls !

Hark ! what shrieking and what yelling
On the midnight wind is swelling,
As each doomed, ill-fated dwelling's
Swept like chaff before the wind ;
With the maddened billows curling,
In the yawning vortex whirling,
Down the long dark valley hurling,
Leaving nought but wreck behind.

Morning dawns on desolation ;
From that vale of tribulation
Rises wailful lamentation

For the hundreds cold and dead.
  Here a father and a mother,
  There a sister and a brother,
  Arms entwined around each other,
Lying stark and stiff a-bed.

  Lonely hearts are sadly mourning
  Dearest friends no more returning,
But we cannot bring the lives back that are gone.
  Let us sympathize by giving
  Something to assist the living
Who are homeless in the valley of the Don.

———o———

WRECK OF THE *NAPOLEON*.[1]

By the howling tempest driven,
  Swift the darksome rain-clouds sweep
O'er the scowling midday heaven ;
  And on beach and craggy steep
Break the great sea-billows with a dreadful roar,
    And in clouds of starry spray,
    In the elemental fray,
    They are blown from out the bay
          Far ashore.

Through the drizzly rain and mist,
  Where the billows wild and dark

[1] A Swedish vessel lost some years ago, with all hands, on the Fife-
shire coast. Although there was a lifeboat stationed close to the scene
of the disaster, no attempt was made to succour the crew, and the
conduct of those in charge was severely animadverted upon by the
public press.

By the trailing clouds are kissed,
   Dimly 'pears a fated bark,
Drifting shoreward, swift and helpless, through the
   gloom ;
         Now her bulwarks high she rears,
         Now she well-nigh disappears,
         As the rugged coast she nears
               To her doom.

No power can now retard
   Her inevitable fate,
And the winds and waves regard
   Not the seamen's cries,—too late !—
As athwart the rocks and breakers shoots her bow
         With a loud and dismal dash,
         While her yielding timbers crash,
         And the white-tipped billows lash
               Stern and prow.

Now the seamen trembling stand
   On the shrouds, and wailing shrieks
For assistance come to land,
   Where a crowd, with tear-wet cheeks,
Line the rocky sea-beach, gazing sadly on.
         Is there no boat to save ?
         Are there no hearts to brave
         That wild, tempestuous wave ?
               Are there none ?

Weary hours of anguish go,
   Seeming days to them, I ween ;
Dark despair and utter woe
   Fill their souls ; no boat is seen :
With the daylight dies the hope that help will come.

On eternity's dim verge
They are ling'ring, whilst the surge
And the winds a mournful dirge
        Weirdly hum.

From the lurching vessel's side,
    See, despairingly, a form
Leaps into the cruel tide ;
    Oh, may He who rules the storm
Guide him safely o'er the billows to the shore !
        Now to swim in vain he tries,
        Whilst the salt waves choke his sighs,
        In the dark he sinks to rise
            Never more.

Daylight merges into shade,
    And more piteous and shrill
Wax their hopeless calls for aid ;
    Now with rigid limbs and chill,
One by one they drop, to perish in the gloom.
        A short struggle, then repose
        From life's weary toils and woes,
        And the cold, dark waters close
            O'er their tomb.

On Scandinavia's strand,
    By the stormy North Sea main,
Weary hearts may watching stand ;
    They will watch, alas, in vain
For the dear ones that will never come to land.
        By the rugged Fifan shore,
        Where the North Sea breakers roar,
        Sound they sleep to wake no more,
            Hapless band !

LINES ON LEAVING SCOTLAND.

SCOTLAND, loved land, farewell !
Thy hallowed, rock-bound shores to fade begin ;
    The foaming billows swell
Without, my heart with anguish swells within,
To think that ere to-morrow's sun shall light
The heavens, thou'rt hid for ever from my sight.

'Tis hard from home to part,
'Tis sad to leave the friends we love behind ;
    For, oh, the weary heart
In dreams of wealth no soothing balm can find,
No gleam of joy the troubled soul to cheer,
No kindly word to stay the farewell tear !

In youth's bright, joyous dreams,
I've roamed in childish gladness through thy dells ;
    And from thy silvery streams
Oft I have culled the pearly, shining shells ;
I've watched the rushing cascade's glittering spray
Mimic in glory's hues the bow of day.

What though no palm trees rise,
In feathery splendour waving on thy air,
    Telling of bright blue skies,
And birds of rainbowed plumage rich and rare ?
Upon thy hills, o'er martyr-warriors' graves,
The heather-bell in silence sweetly waves.

Thy heaven-kissed mountains hoar
Rear their huge forms magnificently grand ;
    Where the loud tempests roar,

In sombre, sullen solitude they stand,
Where the proud eagle soars in wild delight,
Careering far above the storm's giant might.

Land of the mighty brave,
Who fought on many a blood-red battle plain
To earn a glorious grave,
Or rid thy shores of tyranny's dark chain,—
Famed Bannockburn and Stirling Bridge can tell
How well thy sons have fought, how nobly fell !

Scotland, I leave thy shore,
The bark bounds swiftly o'er the swelling foam ;
Farewell for evermore !
In a far land I seek another home.
Dear land of mountain, muirland, lake, and river,
While memory lives, forget thee I can never !

———o———

A CONFLAGRATION IN THE CITY.

THE city's labour-wheels are silent now,
The weary rest from life's tumultuous fight,
The cares that cloud the toil-worn workman's brow
Fade 'midst the balmy slumbers of the night.

Upon the death-like stillness breaks no sound,
Save the low sigh of breezes chill and damp,
And the night watchmen, on their lonely rounds,
Pacing along with slow and measured tramp.

But hark ! a sudden startling clank of bells
  Peals through the dull and misty morning sky,
Sharper and louder growing. Ah ! it tells
  In ominous sounds of conflagration nigh.

And the night watchmen, anxious and amazed,
  Stand by the doorways of the sleeping town,
Gazing with eager looks around. Now's raised
  The dreadful cry, Fire ! fire ! far up and down.

When sudden storms arise, as the first rush
  Of billows breaks upon a still sea-shore,
So breaks upon the grey dawn's solemn hush
  The noisy tumult, and the rush and roar

Of fearless firemen goading frighted steeds,
  That drag the red fire-engines swift along ;
A cloud of dark-brown smoke, uprising, leads
  To the dread scene the expectant, eager throng.

The goal is reached. God ! 'tis a fearful sight !
  From the long rows of windows, smoke and flames,
Commingled, roar and burst with awful might ;
  But hark ! a loud and dismal crash proclaims

The roof has sunk ; a momentary hush
  Reigns over all, while up the lurid sky
Dense smoky volumes darkly roll and rush,
  While far along red meteors flash and fly.

As after lulls more fiercely than before
  The tempest howls, so now the mighty waves
Of flame with tenfold vigour whirl and roar,
  Like the sea's hollow boom in ocean caves.

G

Onward the fiery breakers roll amain,
  Leaving pale desolation in their track,
Till all is wrapt in one wild sea of flame,
  And left a smoking, mouldering, dismal wrack.

Mankind, such is your fate !   To-day ye stand
  Erect in all the pride of youthful bloom ;
To-morrow levelled by the unseen hand
  Of death, then laid to moulder in the tomb.

Whilst from these blackened ruins, smouldering,
  A building more majestic may arise,
So may a grander, nobler body spring
  From the cold dust of man that lowly lies.

Ballads, Lively and Serious.

BALLADS, LIVELY AND SERIOUS.

A TALE OF HORROR.

THE night was dark, the wind blew wild, in torrents fell
    the rain,
The thunder bellowed loudly, and the lightning flashed
    amain ;
While tired and hungry, cold and wet, with spirits far from
    light,
I trudged along in hopes to find a shelter for the night.

I travelled on and on,—it was a lonely road, I ween ;
Full many a league I'd gone, but ne'er a dwelling had I
    seen,—
Till, wearied out and hopeless, I sank down, when, welcome
    sight !
Through the thick darkness I descried a glimmering ray
    of light.

With hope renewed, I tottered on until I reached the spot
From whence the light proceeded,—'twas a gloomy-looking
    cot ;
I sought the door, and was about to knock, when, lo, within
Arose loud shrieks and horrid screams, and dreadful noise
    and din.

I started back affrighted, while amazement filled my soul ;
Then cautiously I crept to where the light shone through a
    bole,
And, peering in, upon my wondering eyes there burst a view
So horrible, it froze my blood, and thrilled me through and
    through.

Two men were there, fit hands they seemed to take a human
    life :
One stood with visage ghastly, while he clutched a bloody
    knife ;
The other knelt, and held the victim down with all his force,
Till all grew still, and on the gory ground there lay a corse !

In fear and terror, from the awful scene I turned and fled,
Through wind and rain ; my only thought was to avenge
    the dead :
At length I reached a little town, then straightway to the jail
I went, and sought a constable, and told my tragic tale.

At once a gig was hired ; then back we drove with lightning
    speed,
Until we reached the cot where had transpired the horrid
    deed.
Extinguished was the light, and all was dark and still within,
But soon we roused the inmates up, and boldly entered in.

I knew the villains at a glance ; quite thunderstruck stood
    they,
Till one spoke up, 'I'd like to know your business here, I
    pray ?'
'Quite soon enough you'll know,' I said; 'but not to hinder
    time,
We take you into custody charged with a dreadful crime.'

'A dreadful crime!' they both exclaimed, with faces
    ghastly white ;
'There's some mistake.' 'Perhaps there is,' I said ; 'but
    fetch a light,
That we may search your premises, and very soon we'll show
There's not the least mistake, which you so well already
    know.'

'Oh, welcome, certainly,' they said, 'if that is your desire.'
So then we searched the barn in vain, and then went to
    the byre,
And there, stretched on a board that lay on the red sodden
    ground,
The object of our search, rolled in a crimsoned cloth, was
    found.

'Ha, villains!' I exclaimed, 'behold your victim, pale and
    cold !'
While tremblingly I knelt the blood-stained covering to
    unfold,
And soon exposed to view—oh, heaven ! methinks I see
    it now—
The naked, full-grown carcase of a beautiful fat sow !

Crestfallen and ashamed, I rose and slunk towards the door,
Convulsed with laughter stood the men, the 'bobby' cursed
    and swore ;
Then to the village back we drove, through rain and mirk
    and mire,
But, sad to say, I had to pay ten shillings for the hire !

——0——

NANCY HALL'S GHOST.

A LEGEND OF CULLERCOATS.

COME, all you hardy fishermen, who brave the stormy wind
In search of haddocks, cod, and skate, and fish of every
    kind ;
Draw near, and close attention give to me, while I rehearse
As sad a tale, I'm almost sure, as e'er was told in verse.

In Cullercoats not long ago a fisher lad did dwell,
And if you want his name to know, they called him Geordy
    Bell ;
He was as stout and smart a lad as ever cast a line
To hook the silvery fish that sport amongst the cool sea
    brine.

Next door to him a damsel lived, her name was Nancy Hall,
She baited hooks upon the beach, and was well known to all ;
Though you might walk for days along an unfrequented way,
You would not meet a finer maid than her, I'm safe to say.

So, nothing wonderful to state, this lovely female fell
Right over head and ears in love with handsome Geordy
    Bell ;
But Geordy, cruel, saucy lad, was of a fickle mind,
To love young Nancy in return he felt noways inclined.

One summer night along the sands this worthy couple
    strayed,
Said she, 'O Geordy love, you know I'm but a lonely maid,
And I have often thought within myself that you and me
Would look as well, if we were wed, as many whom I see.'

Young Geordy silent stood awhile, then coughed and blew
    his nose,
And answered, 'You are wrong if for one moment you
    suppose
That I would lower my dignity to wed the likes of you ;
Oh no ! if that's your little game, proud Nancy Hall,
    adieu.'

'Oh, cruel man ! ere you depart, come list to me and
    weep,
Before I throw my body in the cold and briny deep ;'
But, heedless of her words, young Geordy homeward
    quickly sped,
Quite careless whether she came after him alive or dead.

'Woe's me !' she cried, and wrung her hands ; 'my heart
    is broken quite,
I feel it is impossible to live another night !'
So then she laid her down upon the sand beside the sea,
And, sobbing, moaned, 'Oh, kindly waves, dash quickly
    over me !'

She lay perhaps an hour or more in silence on the sand,
Expecting that the waves would come and wash her off the
    land ;
But when at length, with waiting tired, she turned her head
    about,
She saw, instead of coming in, the tide was running out.

'Alas, alas ! I thought to die, yet save myself the sin,
But I'll come back to-morrow when the tide is coming in.'
So home she went, but there she found her love had sailed
    away,
In quest of haddocks, cod, and ling, far out across the bay.

While he was lying snugly in the boat at dead of night,
Thinking he had not done with her exactly what was right,
Lo, from the gloomy deep arose on his astonished view
A female form, with flowing hair and robes of snowy hue.

' Oh, fickle, faithless man,' she cried, in tones which well
    he knew,
· Look up, behold the ghost of one who died for love of you !
My body now lies cold and stark among the seaweed green,
And never more upon the sand together we'll be seen.

' But since in life, false-hearted fool, you spurned me for
    your bride,
In death you'll be my bridegroom now below the roaring
    tide.'
So then she tried to drag him forth, but Geordy offered fight,
When instantly she vanished in a brilliant flash of light.

Next evening, as the sun went down, he landed into port,
The boxes and the creels all full of fish of every sort ;
Yet he felt sad at heart, and on his cheek there stood a tear,
To think that Nancy's voice no more would hail him from
    the pier.

But from the boat he saw a crowd collected on the shore,
And in the midst four men upon their shoulders something
    bore ;
He cried, while pale as death he turned, ' Her body they
    have found ;
I'll go and kiss her lips before they lay her in the ground.'

He rushed amongst the crowd, but soon in horror back he
    shrunk,
For there upon a shutter lay young Nancy Hall *dead drunk !*

So, quite disgusted, quickly to a spirit-bar he went,
And drank till every copper that belonged to him was spent.

So now my tale is ended, but before I say farewell,
I think, kind reader, you would like to know if Geordy Bell
Did ever wed young Nancy Hall : I've only got to say
He did ; and if they are not dead, they're living to this day.

———o———

FAITHLESS MOLLY LUKE.

(A RECITATION FOR CHRISTMAS AND NEW YEAR FESTIVE
MEETINGS.)

CHAPTER I.

I ONCE did court a young fair maid, her name was Molly
Luke,
Into a large establishment the victuals she did cook ;
Her face it was the handsomest I ever yet have seen,
And she did always keep herself respectable and clean.

Her waist it was so slender, and her nose it was so taper,
I once did write a poem on her, and sent it to this paper,
But I suspect that to the 'Balaam Box' it was committed ;
If so, confound the editor—his taste is to be pitied.

This maid she was more dear to me than money, clothes,
or food,
To live without her in this world I felt I never could ;
I would have run quite cheerfully through water, wood, or
fire,
In any way to serve or gratify her least desire.

Four times a week I walked eight miles to see this lovely
    maid,
For thunder, lightning, hail, or snow I never felt afraid ;
And she would always welcome me with smiles so bright
    and sunny,
I do declare, without a joke, it made me feel quite funny.

And I would sit beside her with my arms round her waist,
While on the table always sat things pleasant to the taste,—
Boiled ham and chicken, puddings, pies, and roast meat
    nice and brown,
With oceans of the best T.B. to wash them quickly down.

And when the people of the house had all gone off to sleep,
Into the garden silently as ‘ mices ’ we would creep,
And underneath the tall fruit trees a quiet walk we’d take,
And I would kiss her o’er and o’er—’twas good, there’s no
    mistake.

But most of all, how pleasant and delightful ’twas to pull
The various kinds of fruit until my pockets were quite full ;
And then to rest beside her in the shady summer-seat,
And tell her gentle tales of love, while all the while I’d eat !

Oh, cruel fate ! too soon, alas, my dream of bliss was ended !
Some way, I don’t know how it was, this maiden I offended,
And so, to be revenged, she badly used and slighted me,
For full particulars of which the second chapter see.

CHAPTER II.

One evening at the close of day, with spirits light and free,
I went, as was my usual way, dear Molly Luke to see,

And there, beside the table, in mine old accustomed seat,
Another young man snugly sat, devouring bread and meat.

Like one amazed, I stood and gazed at this unwelcome sight
(I felt some queer, you may be sure, as truly well I might);
'Tell me,' I cried, 'what brings that low-bred, sponging
    fellow here,
To eat up all the victuals and to drink up all the beer?'

Upspoke false Molly Luke, 'What right have you to
    interfere?
Too long already *you* have come to court for bread and
    beer;
Then let me tell you, once for all, I've found another beau,
So you had better take the hint, and homeward quickly go.'

'You surely don't mean this?' I cried. She answered, 'Yes,
    I do.'
'Then, Molly Luke, false female, you have broke my heart
    in two.'
Quite overcome with sorrow, I sat down beside the table,
And then began to eat and drink as hard as I was able.

I cleared the plates, then lit my pipe to have a quiet smoke,
When, hark! a sound of feet without the solemn silence
    broke.
'It is the missus,' Molly cried, her visage pale with fear;
'Go, hide at once, or I am lost, if she should find you here.'

My rival to a cupboard ran, while, like a quadruped,
I crawled in on my hands and knees to hide below the bed;
When, sad to say, just as the missus came within the door,
Something—I don't know what it was—I straightway
    tumbled o'er.

'Dear help me, Molly Luke,' she cried, 'what dreadful
    noise is that?'
'I'm sure I cannot tell you, ma'am, unless it is the cat.'
Then all at once she took a thought to look below the bed,
Where I in fear and trembling lay all silent as the dead.

She bolted from the kitchen, bawling, 'Murder! thieves!
    and p'leece!'
To tell the truth, I felt most anxious to 'depart in peace;
So from my hiding-place I crawled, and, with one fearful
    bound,
Leapt through an open window in the hopes to reach the
    ground.

Alas for human hopes! just right below the window stood
A cistern full of water, which was neither clean nor good;
So, with a loud and horrid plunge, headlong I tumbled in,
Without a moment's warning to repent a single sin.

I struggled long and hard for life, as you may well suppose,
The water gushed in torrents down my throat and up my
    nose;
But soon I grew insensible to sorrow, grief, or pain,
And long it was before that I was brought to life again.

MORAL.

Now all you young unmarried men, take warning by my
    tale,
And never go to court young maids alone for cake and ale;
For if you do, it's possible like me some day you'll rue it,
Therefore, to finish up, I say, take my advice—*Don't do it!*

GRIZZEL GOW.

A LAMENTABLE TALE.

Introductory Note.—The incidents brought to light in the following verses are strictly authentic. The story is a beautiful illustration of the deceitful manners and changeable nature of the female portion of the community, and is a solemn warning to them all to beware of trifling with the gentle and affectionate hearts of the male species, to whom I have the honour to belong. When this poem is pathetically rendered, it never fails to draw tears from the hardest hearts. I had the pleasure, not long since, of reciting it before a company of two respectable females, who happened to be busy peeling onions, and ere I was half done there wasn't a dry eye in the whole of the audience assembled, not so much as one. I could quote numerous instances of the powerful effect of the poem on the human feelings, but as I would scorn to utter one syllable in mine own praise, I add no more, and proceed to business.

YOUNG swains and youthful females, aged women and old
    men,
Come hearken to the details of this story from my pen ;
If you're susceptible to tears, prepare to weep them now,
While I relate the melancholy tale of Grizzel Gow.

This charming maid a female was, which no one can deny ;
Upon her stocking soles she stood five feet six inches high ;
The years of her existence numbered two times half-a-score,
While she did weigh eleven stone, or something less or
    more.

And at the time my sad and dismal story does begin,
She earned her bread as barmaid in a rural village inn,
Where her familiar winning ways, and bright, love-beaming
    face,
Had turned the heads of half the males that stayed about
    the place.

But there was one particularly, a baker to his trade,
As smart a lad as ever fired a batch of wheaten bread ;
His age I don't remember, but his name was Simon Giles,
On him young Grizzel did bestow her most bewitching
    smiles.

And he did love her in return far dearer than his life,
And he had vowed to wed her when he took himself a wife.
Vain, foolish dream ! 'the course of true love never did
    run smooth,'
Which Simon to his cost found out, poor love-bewildered
    youth.

One night as usual he dropped in to have his drop of beer,
And to enjoy the company of her he held so dear,
When to his horror and surprise, lo, what did Simon see,
But Grizzel, quite contented, seated on a young man's knee !

Serene and calm and silent he surveyed the guilty pair,
Then in a whisper shouted, 'Villain, knave, what dost thou
    there ?
And thou, false, fickle, base, deceitful, hollow-hearted maid,
I'll be revenged, as sure as I'm a baker to my trade !'

He rushed up to the fireplace, seized the poker in his hand,
Then to his rival gave the tongs, and bawled out, 'Traitor,
    stand !

Defend thy life ! There's nought but blood this insult can
    wipe out !'
But in an instant to the door his rival took the rout.

' Ha! coward, art thou fled?' he cried, when, with a dreadful
    knock,
He smashed the looking-glass to spunks, and then the
    eight-day clock ;
He kicked the table over, broke a globe of golden fishes,
Then haul'd an oaken cupboard down, choke full of china
    dishes ;

Then bounded straightway to the bar, amongst the stock-
    in-trade, -
And every liquor cask and jar low in the dust he laid ;
Likewise each glass and tumbler, jug and bottle too, he
    shatter'd,
And all the contents of the till about the floor he scatter'd.

' Behold,' he cried, 'the dire results of your deceitful ways !
To finish up, I'll hang myself, and end my wretched days !
My ghost shall haunt you while I live ; farewell ! false Grizzel
    Gow,'
Then rush'd into the street like an infuriated cow.

He tore the sign-board to the ground, smash'd every pane
    of glass,
Then madly bolted off to do the fatal deed, alas !
He stole a clothes rope from a green, and tied it to a tree,
And with the loose end round his neck he let himself go
    free.

That night as faithless Grizzel Gow lay sound asleep in bed,
She saw a tall white figure standing close beside her head ;

It froze her blood, and filled her soul with horror and
    affright,
To gaze upon this tall unearthly figure clad in white ;
As nearer still it came, with glassy eyes upon her fixt,
It cried, with hollow voice, ' To be continued in our next !'

————o————

LINES TO SUSAN.

BY HER LOVE-SICK SWAIN.

O SUSAN ! pretty dove, I love you dearly—
    So dearly that I cannot live without you
Much longer ; for, to tell the truth, I'm nearly,
    If not entirely, crazy all about you,
For day and night continually I'm musing
Upon your charms, dear, blooming, bright-eyed Susan.

You are a beauty, no mistake about it ;
    I can't find one to match you ; and I'm willing,
If any persons—male or female—doubt it,
    To stake one silver sixpence to a shilling,
That they may search through Hebburn, Shields, and
    Jarrow,
And Monkton too, in vain to find your marrow.

Your charms, in fact, are quite beyond description ;
    I sometimes think you an unearthly being,—
One of those fairy creatures which in fiction
    We often read of, but are never seeing :
But what of that ? Your charms avail me little,
For me you do not care one single spittle.

Completely to a skeleton I'm wasting,
    Each day I know myself a great deal thinner ;

No wonder, scarce a bit of food I'm tasting
  At either breakfast, supper, tea, or dinner ;
And this, alas ! is all through you refusing
To be my better half, O cruel Susan !

I've striven hard, tho' vainly, to forget you ;
  But this I know, I cannot strive much longer.
I wish to goodness I had never met you,
  For now I would have been a great deal stronger
But as it is, I feel as weak as water,
And not a thing but love with me the matter.

I'm wretched, miserable, sad, and lonely,
  I have no pleasure in my life whatever ;
I see no other remedy, but only
  To go and toss myself into the river ;
Only it is so cold, I don't know whether
To go just now, or wait till warm weather.

I do believe before a month is over,—
  Unless on me, dear Susan, you take pity,—
That the long grass my poor remains will cover
  In some lone rural churchyard in the city.
Then be my wife at once, sweet Susan, can't you,
Or else, both day and night, my ghost will haunt you.

———o———

LOVE'S TRIUMPH.

A SEQUEL TO ' LINES TO SUSAN.'

DEAR SUSAN, I am come to take
  A final leave of you at last ;
And oh, I think my heart will break,
  Since all my dreams of bliss are past !

I had my mind made up to die,
  Since you with me refused to wed ;
But second thoughts are best, and I
  Intend to emigrate instead.

I've just come through from Glasgow town,
  The port from which I mean to sail,
I've paid my passage money down,—
  But why, O Susan, turn so pale ?

A week to-day I sail away
  Across the blue Atlantic main ;
And I'm afraid, sweet lovely maid,
  We've little chance to meet again.

And, Susan dear, I do not doubt,
  When I am far removed from here,
That you will often think about
  My lonely lot, and shed a tear.

But happy here I might have been
  Through all my future years of life,
If you had only clearly seen
  Your way to be my wedded wife.

But ere I go I wish to make
  A present of this photograph ;
I hope you'll keep it for my sake,
  Since you won't be my better half.

And now, to soothe my wounded soul,
  Give me one kiss before we part :
There, that will do.   Farewell ! adieu !
  Dear idol of my youthful heart !

　　·　　·　　·　　·　·　　·　　·　　·

And so you mean to emigrate ?
  Ah, well, one word before you go :
In justice I but wish to state—
  What every man like you should know—

That we in courtship often mean
  The quite reverse of what we say ;
A blind and simple fool you've been,—
  There, take my hand, and name the day !

———*o*———

LUCY LEE :

A LEGEND OF THE TYNE.

I ONE time knew a damsel fair,
  Her name was Lucy Lee,
As smart a lass, I do declare,
  As one would wish to see.

Into a dwelling-house she stayed
  Near by the Felling shore ;
And, oh ! she was a nice young maid,
  As I've remark'd before.

Young Lucy Lee a sweetheart had,
  They called him Billy Coots ;
He was as brisk and bold a lad
  As ever walk'd in boots.

And he to earn an honest crust
  Did plough the coaly Tyne,—

A line of business which I trust
   And hope will ne'er be mine.

One night this couple went to walk,
   As lovers often will,
To have a confidential talk
   O'er things in general.

'Dear Lucy Lee, my love,' said he,
   'To-morrow I must go
And plough the waves to Hebburn quay,
   Whatever winds may blow.

'Before I go I wish to learn
   One single thing or two :
I calculate that you discern
   My heart is fixed on you.

'Now, you will swear by all that's fair
   That you'll be true to me,
Until I do return to you
   From far-off Hebburn quay.'

· Dear Lucy Lee she wept and sighed,
   And cried, 'O darling Bill,
I swear to be your loving bride ;
   Yes, blow me, but I will.'

Then Billy caught her to his heart,
   'That's settled now,' he said ;
'My life's pole-star, adieu ! we part,'
   Then home he went to bed.

Next morning early he set sail,
   When, lo ! a blast arose,
Which blew the keel head over heel,
   And drowned all Billy's clothes.

Quite destitute, all bruised and cut,
   He on a rock was hurl'd,
Without a bit of food, and not
   A copper in the world.

When tidings of this sad affair
   Came home to Lucy Lee,
She tore her hands and wrung her hair,
   Crying, ' Goodness gracious me !

' The dire effects of this great blow
   I never will recover ;
I may as well prepare to go
   And join my faithful lover.'

She took a tender leave of all
   Her friends and kindred too,
Then went and squared up any small
   Accounts which she was due ;

Then walked away quite calm and cool
   Until she reached the river,
And plunged into a shallow pool
   Without a single shiver.

It came to pass that very night
   Young Billy did arrive,
A friendly keel had hove in sight,
   And picked him up alive.

And like a clap of thunder fell
 The tidings on his ear :
He stood and gazed like one half crazed
 With drinking rum and beer.

He threw himself upon the floor,
 And ne'er a word could speak,
Till they brought whisky, which he swore
 Felt most confounded weak ;

Then cried, 'In life we two were one,
 The same in death we'll be,'
Then to the river shore he ran,
 In search of Lucy Lee.

He wandered up, and wandered down,
 Till, lo ! he did behold
Young Lucy in her bathing gown,
 All shivering in the cold ;

And fairly overcome with joy,
 He kissed his love and said,
'I'll bet a quart, no more we part
 Until that we are wed.'

———0———

WEE RICHIE, THE MILL LADDIE.

TH' snaw-flakes frae the wintry cluds
 Fa' heavily and chill,
As puir wee Richie, scant o' duds,
 Gangs trudgin' frae th' mill.

Wi' bitter grief his heart is rent,
　The tears gush doon his cheek ;
For some sma' faut the loon 's been sent
　Anither job to seek.

He's fearin' hame to gang, but, ah !
　Nae hame nor freends has he ;
His mither sleeps beneath th' snaw,
　His father i' th' sea.

His little brithers Tam and Jock
　Lie cauld wi' sister Nell ;
And now he bides 'mang stranger folk,
　An orphan by himsel'.

Oh, wearily through ilka street
　He wanders up and doon,
Amang the bitin', blindin' sleet,
　That's driftin' a' aroun' !

His hackit feet sae cauld an' weet,
　Wae's me ! th' orphan loon,
Withoot a hame, withoot a freend,
　In a' the big mill toon.

But noo 'tis late, and quenched the licht
　Which did the lang streets fill ;
He wonders whaur he'll pass the nicht,
　The nicht sae mirk and chill.

Into an eerie close he creeps,
　And on a darksome stair
He sits him doon, the puir wee loon,
　His heart baith sad and sair.

And on his knees to God abune
  He breathes a simple prayer,
He learn'd in happy days bygane
  Under a mither's care.

He lays him doon, cauld an' forlorn,
  But sleeps nae lang nor soun';
He's up and aff at early morn,
  The mills to gang the roun'.

Three weary days he tramps aboot,
  And pleads for wark in vain ;
Three langsome nichts he sleeps thereoot,
  His wee limbs racked in pain.

There's ne'er a bit has cross'd his mou',
  To beg or steal he'd scorn ;
For actions honest, just, and true,
  The laddie's life adorn.

The gloamin' o' th' third lang day
  To dark has deepened doon,
While dreamily his dreary way
  He wanders through th' toon.

His looks sae wae, and cheeks sae pale,
  Whaur roses ance did dwell,
Silent bespeak the mournfu' tale
  His tongue it winna tell.

• Mair wild and luminous grows th' licht
  That's glintin' in his een,
Just like twa starns blinkin' bricht
  Far in the blue serene.

A numb and weary faintness steals
  Owre a' th' laddie's frame,
He glances up to heaven, and feels
  A langin' to be hame.

.   .   .   .

The factory toon is hush'd ance mair
  In slumbers still and deep ;
Again upon a cauld damp stair
  He's shiv'rin' gane to sleep.

In dreams his sainted mither's voice
  Falls sweetly on his ear ;
It tells him o' calm heavenly joys,
  And whispers they are near.

His lanely heart o' grief and pain
  Is freed for evermair,
While comes a saft and joyous strain
  O' music through the air.

A vision bricht bursts on his sicht :
  The wintry cluds are riven,
And clad in robes o' silv'ry licht
  The angels come frae heaven.

They bear his spirit hame to dwell
  Whaur tears the een ne'er dim ;
The clinkin' o' th' lood mill bell
  Nae mair will wauken him.

———o·———

THE MIDNIGHT SPECTRE.

WHILE sound asleep in bed the other night,
   I was aroused by something loudly calling;
I started up, and, lo ! upon my sight
   There burst a vision horrid and appalling.

Before me stood a figure dark and tall,
   With visage grim and ghastly and repulsive,
Holding a lamp that shed upon the wall
   A strange, uncertain light : I felt convulsive.

I heard afar a solemn-sounding bell
   The mournful, mystic hour of midnight pealing,—
To me it sounded like my own death knell;
   My limbs grew powerless, and my brain was reeling.

Trembling, I cried, 'Strange visitant, why come
   At this lone hour to haunt a sinful mortal?
Tell me, are you of earth, or are you from
   Beyond the confines of the grave's dark portal ?'

The spectre made reply, 'While in the street
   I took a fancy to survey the landing :
Beg pardon, sir, I'm "bobby" on this beat ;
   I found your lobby door wide open standing.'

———0———

A NEW YEAR'S DAY.

IT fell on the first days of the year,
　　That hallowed time of joy and mirth,
When dear ones gather from far and near
　　Together around the social hearth ;

When bitter feelings are all forgot,
　　And friend greets friend with a love sincere,
I spent afar, in a rural cot,
　　The holidays to all so dear.

A rural cot, in a sheltered spot,
　　Far from the factory town's uproar,
With a tall hedge round a little plot
　　Of garden land before the door;

And where, in the bright, glad summer time,
　　Over the walls the sweet woodbine,
And the honeysuckle, and wild rose climb,
　　And the birds and the bees make song divine.

But then the flowers lay withered and chill,
　　The tall hedgerow stood black and bare ;
The bird on the leafless bough sat still,
　　The bee had gone I know not where,—

As round the fireside, warm and bright,
　　Sat we all in the morning tide,
Our hearts aglow with calm delight,
　　And toil and care all cast aside.

And there sat Mary, of laughing mood,
　　And brown-eyed Janet, so frank and free,
And their loving mother, so kind and good ;
　　And we were glad as we could be.

The virgin snow clad field and hill,
　　The landscape all around lay bleak ;
The birds came nigh to the window-sill,
　　Shelter to find, and food to seek.

The blackbird, robin, and sparrow came
　　To pick the crumbs dear Janet threw out ;
The pitiless storm had made them tame—
　　Poor wee things, how they hopped about !

But though all things without looked bleak,
　　The flowers of joy bloomed bright within ;
And Mary sang with a voice so sweet,
　　It made our hearts throb all akin.

Our thoughts went back to happier years,
　　To years when our sun of childhood shone
And our eyes filled with the warm salt tears,
　　As we spake of the days for ever gone,

And the hallowed scenes for ever past,
　　And the joys that left behind no pain ;
The pleasures, all too pure to last,
　　We never on earth can feel again.

And thus, with many a smile and sigh,
　　We passed the pleasant time away,
Till to the little town hard by
　　We thought to go and spend the day.

So, arm in arm, and side by side,
   Away went Mary and Janet and I,
Over the snow in the morning tide ;
   And we were a merry company.

We cared not for the snow or the wet,
   But gaily on to the town we went ;
And I never, never can forget
   The happy day which there we spent.

We thought not of returning home
   Till over all the dark came down,
And the golden stars i' the deep blue dome
   Shóne over the white-roofed little town.

And, like the beacon lights of old,
   The pit-fires gleamed with a ruddy glow,—
Gleamed far over the snow-clad wold,
   As merrily homeward we did go.

And after many a pleasant chat
   And merry laugh, we reached once more
The rustic cot with the tiny plot
   Of garden ground before the door.

And there we sat in the firelight flush,
   And laughed and sang till the echoes sweet
Rang through the calm and solemn hush
   Of the hours when night and morning meet.

Amidst the world's sad toil and strife,
   How dear to us such joys as these !
They cheer us on the voyage of life,
   And lighten all its miseries.

Like golden sun-gleams here and there
    Upon a gloomy, trackless sea,
Or oasis in a desert bare,
    They live within the memory.

———o———

A TALE OF MYSTERY.

GOOD people all, who in large towns like bees do
    congregate,
And ye who unfrequented rural districts habitate,
And ye who plough the briny seas a livelihood to earn,
Ho ! one and all, draw near to me, a solemn lesson learn.

Be very silent and give ear, speak not one single word,
While I relate the saddest tale that never yet occurred,—
A most disastrous circumstance which lately since
    befell
Two very nice young people, that I knew extremely
    well.

One of this couple was a damsel graceful, tall, and
    slender,
In fact, a first-class sample of the gentle female gender ;
I'm safe to state no flower that ever bloom'd in field or
    garden
Was half so fair as this young maid ; but if I'm wrong,
    beg pardon.

And, nothing strange, she loved a youth, so handsome,
    gay, and gallant,
A well-bred, wealthy person, with a great amount of
    talent ;

Upon the whole, to speak the truth without exaggeration,
A finer pair 'twere hard to find in all the wide creation.

But, lack-a-day! the tragic fate of these unlucky creatures,
Which presently I will relate with all its horrid features,
Was dismal, dark, and melancholy far beyond description ;
But facts, I calculate you know, are stranger far than
    fiction.

I'll lay my life so sad a tale you never yet did hear ;
'Twill make you stare with blank surprise, and quake
    with downright fear,
The grey hairs on your hoary head will quickly rise on end,
When you the awful nature of my story comprehend.

With sorrow, grief, and pity it will melt the hardest soul,
And cause the briny teardrops down your wrinkled
    cheeks to roll,
Like showers of rain in summer from a clear blue frosty
    sky,
Or water from a public well which happens to be dry ;

'Twill make the blood through all your veins to circulate
    quite cold,
While I the awful horrors of this tragic tale unfold ;
You'll all bawl out with one loud thundering voice when
    I am done,
So foul a business never was transacted 'neath the sun !

It fell upon a day, a day to be remembered long
By generations yet unborn, in story and in song,
This deed, so fraught with horror as to strike the boldest
    dumb,—
This deed,— but, friends, excuse me, I am fairly overcome.

I

I'll be compelled, both sad to say and painful to remark,
To leave you all at present most completely in the dark ;
But if I live, and keep my health, perhaps some other day
I will conclude this doleful tale—quite possible I may.

————o————

THE WEEPING MAIDEN.

MAIDEN, pray tell me why those tears
   Do sparkle in thine eyes,
And wet thy cheeks? oh, say what fears
   Within thy heart arise?

Have friends proved false, or has some foe
   Traduced thy stainless fame ?
Or has the hand of fate laid low
   Some friend who bears thy name ?

Or has some loved one, dearer still,
   Thy trusting heart betrayed ?
Why do those tears thine eyelids fill ?
   What ails thee, fair young maid ?

Alas ! kind sir, but if you must
   Have me to tell the reason,
I'm after peeling onions, just
   A mutton chop to season.

Lyrical Rhymes.

LYRICAL RHYMES.

THE BAIRNIES AT HAME.

THE bricht sun o' summer sinks grandly to rest
'Mid calm rosy cluds doon the fair gowden west,
The blue hills are glintin' wi' glory arrayed,
Th' bonnie wee birds in th' hawthorn glade
Are carollin' sweetly on ilka green spray,
As hameward I trudge frae th' toils o' th' day.

Far awa' doon i' yon cool mossy dell,
Whaur blossom th' craw-pea and wavin' blue-bell,
And whaur the lang fern creeps the grey rocks amang,
A clear siller burnie rows wimplin' alang :
In a green shady neuk, by its waters sae bricht,
Stands the snug cosy biggin' sae dear to my sicht.

Just noo its low rooftree, close theekit wi' straw,
To keep us a' warm when the winter winds blaw,
Keeks through th' thick foliage, sae welcome to view,
While frae th' lum-head the reek curls up sae blue ;
Ha ! the wee tots are crossin' th' brig owre th' stream,
To welcome their dad to his love-lichtit hame.

Oh, sweet are th' pleasures th' gloamin'-time brings !
Then love roond oor dwellin' a bricht halo flings,
We a' are sae happy; though frugal oor fare,
We aye are contented, then what need we mair ?
Ony pleasures that wealth gies are no worth th' name,
Compared wi' th' joys 'mang the bairnies at hame.

Hoo cosy we sit roond th' warm ingle-neuk !
Th' totums a' daffin', while I'm at my beuk ;
My dear wifie sits wi' th' wean on her knee,
And croons it to sleep wi' a saft lullaby ;
Or is darnin' a stockin', or steekin' a seam
O' a duddie o' claes for th' bairnies at hame.

Though sair I maun toil frae th' dawnin' to nicht,
My heart is aye cheery, my spirits aye licht ;
I think o' th' weans that ilk turn o' th' plew
Helps to bring a sma' dud, or a bit to th' mou';
I covet nae riches, I envy nae fame,
But strength to provide for th' bairnies at hame.

Nae doot we have had cares and sorrows enoo',
But if life were a' sunshine, oor joys would be few ;
For if winter ne'er cam', wi' its cauld gloomy skies,
We wadna sae dearly the summer-time prize ;
Sae oor joys hae been purer since tearfu' we saw
Oor dear little Archie laid deep 'neath th' snaw.

Sae adoon life's dark stream may we peacefully glide,
My wifie an angel o' love by my side ;
And th' totums—God bless their wee hearties !—I ken
Will grow to be braw bonnie lassies and men ;
But although I sud live till I'm donnart and lame,
I'll aye mind o' th' joys 'mang the bairnies at hame.

ROSALEEN.

SAILING o'er the calm blue sea,
Still my thoughts are all of thee,
Oh, so dear thou art to me!
      Bonnie Rosaleen.
But so lonely here am I,
Darling, thou no longer nigh,
O'er the past I fondly sigh,
      Sweet Rosaleen.

In the lonesome dead of night,
When the stars are gleaming bright,
And the moon's pale mystic light
      Glorifies the scene;
While the lonely deck I pace,
Everywhere thy beauteous face
In the moon and stars I trace,
      Fair Rosaleen.

When I lay me down to rest,
Rock'd upon the ocean's breast,
Comes the hour that I love best,
      Bonnie Rosaleen.
Though the night is wild and drear,
All is bright, for thou art near ;
In my dreams thy voice I hear,
      Dear Rosaleen.

———*o*———

A LUVER'S CATASTROPHY.[1]

A TRUE TAIL.

ONE morning i went out tu take the cool air,
And wauk through the cenery all round about there,
When by a young female cum wauking along,
The finest i ever clapp'd my 2 ise upon.

I hailed her, and said, 'Angel, where are yu goin'
At such an intimious hour all alone?'
She answered and said, 'I'm the meal miler's dater,
Just goin' away for a pale full of water.'

I said, 'Yu're an angel if air there is one,
Yure cheeks are like apels exposd tu the sun,
Yure ankel is the neatest i niver did see,
And white as the fome of the mity salt sea.

'Yure mouth is the sweetest I've yet cumd akross ;
Yure nose, to diskribe it i feel at a loss ;
Yure brow is like chauk, and yure ise is as blue
As the vilet or pansy—i luve you, i du.'

---

[1] In looking over some old MS. lately, I came across this and the two following pieces, which I had given up as being lost to posterity. They were composed during a temporary sojourn in a lunatic asylum. I had some hesitation in giving them a place in this collection, until submitting them to the judgment of a friend, a great 'cricket,' with the result that he considered them superior to anything in the book. This at once decided me, although I must admit that I have fallen at least fifty per cent. in my own estimation as to my qualifications as a rhymer.

2 times then i kist her, saying, ' Deer hivnly kreture,
I gudge by yure looks yu must have a kind nature ;
And if for tu marry yu du feel inklined,
I sware I will have you—cum, make up your mind.'

I kist her twice more, she cried, ' Stop ! what's yure
    game ?'
While over her fase the red blushes did came.
' Yung stranger,' she said, ' yu seam rather abrup—
In such a short time mi mind i can't make up.'

Yet twice more i kist her, then she laid to mine
Her red rosy cheek, and said, ' Take me, i'm thine,
For bad or for evil, for iver and iver,
There is nothing but death can our loving hearts siver.'

By this time us 2 had arrived at the well,
A nice, quiet place in the midst of a dell.
I sade, ' Just alow me yure pitsher tu fill.'
She smilinly ansered, ' Of korse, luve, i will.'

I nelt kamly doun tu fill up my luve's pale ;
In kase i mite fall in she kawt my kote tale,
But all of a suddin, lo ! paneful to tell,
I tumbild head formost into the cold well.

My past life rushed by me—i felt i was lost,
My mind was quite seteled to give up the gost ;
The watir gushd intu my nose, ears, and throte—
But stil my love held by the tale of my kote.

She struggled and shoutit and vilently pulled—
By this time my luve was konsidrably koold.
At last I was draggd out both sadder and wiser,
For the rest of my tail see last ear's *Advertiser*.

ANN ADRESS TWO A WHAIL.

INNTRODUCKTIRRY REMARKS.

The subgek off my mews in this instans Is a Kwadriped
of the fish kind.   it is A veri Kewries & remarkibill inseck
that Kant live on dri Land, end Dize if Kept two long Belo
the watir.   it is awlso a veri intiristing & usefool Anny
Mill, grately attached two its offspring, Butt has nivir Bean
noan 2 beekum dumestikated.   Eye regret much tow sae,
that i nivir Had thee Pleshir off inspecktin wan, unless At
a distans, Butt Ass it was dark at the tyme, I Kan skarsely
speek as two its good Kwalities from persinel observayshin.
The facks brote too lite in the versis belo, r Kulld cheefly
frum Ann old Kolleckshin off munthlie tracks, & docktir
Kuming's Book on Beas, two thee last named ahthir eye
tendir my Great fool thanks, & besides i shawl Bee daylighted
to subskribe my might too the fund for the monymint that
is 2 Bee erecktit two his memiry in 8 teen 60 ate.[1]   As
theas remarks kunklood my observayshins, i proseed with
my adress.

AWAIK, mi mews, ryse frum ure idol slumbirs.
ade Mee two cing inn Sweat, & tunefool Numbirs
2 that Grate wundir Off the Broot Kreeayshin
Whoose naim dus hed mie Pome on this Okayshin.

hale mitey monirk off Thee finny speshis,
The larjist noan of awl the tribe of fishes.
sum idea of yoor sighs is estymaited
When for A solim fack ive hard it stayted

---

[1] Written shortly after his famous prophecy.

that wans upon a tyme sum shipreckd saylirs
whew had Bean lost eye reckin from the whaylirs
Sayleng in Open boates Inn sertch off driland
Diskoverd what thay Took too Bee ann iland
thay landid Bilt a hut, a fire then lited
Butt inn less time than i hav took two rite it
The iland plunged belo the ragin Billys
& the frale mortils fownd kold watry pillys
whyle strugglin for thair lifes thay understandid
It was a sleepin whail on whitch thade landid.

inormis monstir Off the polir rejins
Whair iyery seesin men doo Swarm In leejins
with lanses, speers, harpoons & guns too chase u.
thay are nut the Leest afrade 2 face u
When u r kawt & killed thay taik and skin yew
& thay Doo find Grate stoar off good oil Inn yoo
yoor bons awlso R reckond hyly valibill
Butt for yoor flesh its totilly onsalibill.
Altho ive hard it sed the Eskweymaw
if hungery will devour yoo Up kwite raw.

Huge powerfool Beest, tho' terrybill inn Stature
if Let aloan yoor off a harmliss Nature
But when harpoond blindfold yoo rush On madly
& sumtimes ure remorsliss Fose fair badly ;
With wan stroak Off yoor dredfool Tale, u batter,
Thair bote two match wood, & lyke hale stons skattar
the kroo pell mell into the kold salt watir.

gigantik Broot.   yood maik a Good edishin
2 Mr woomwells wild Beest xhibishin
ide pay 3 Pens yet Studdie dew ekonomy
two feest mie Ise on Sutch A rair fenomony

Within my mind Grate wundir yood awaiken.
ide lyke yoor Cart de viset lyfe sighs taken
twood Hold a promynint plase in 2 my albim
Such fottygraffs eye no r seen Butt celdim.

prodigous Fish. yoor skelletin, if sheetid
With iron.   strongly fixt Bye rivets Heetid.
wood maik A ship kwite larg enuff two Kerry
5 hunder Hewmin beins two broty ferry.

Stewpendys obgek.   travlin ore thee Hie way
ive seen yoor ponderis gaw Bones arch A Buy way.
Ive thote had Samsin when he sloo the Masses
yewsd wan off them & throne aside Thee Asses.
For wan he sloo.   He wood Hav slade a hundred
with sutch A wepin, no one would have wonder'd.

Wild ravenis whail from U may hevin defend us
ure swallowin powers must shoorly Bee tremendis
Sho me the Mann or womin, whig or Torrie
that has Nut red that strange remarkabill storey
How yew did swally up the poor oald profit
Yet aftir Awl no prophet you maid off it
U kept Hymn 3 hole daze within yoo stickin
then spewd him Up again alive & kickin.
How he got down yoor throte two mees a mistery
As i hav Red in gold smiths natril histery.
whitch is Korreck as far as eye kan lern
that yoove Bean chokit Buy a smawl fresh hern
Eye oan this pint rekwires Sum Xplanaishon
i Leeve it two the breetish Asoshyaishin.

———0———

MY FIRST KORTSHIP. A SONG.

AIR—THE LAIRD OH KOCKPEN.

IT hapind exackly just 5 years kum joon,
I went out to rambel wan fine afternoon,
Of the fresh air to drink inn a mowthfull or 2,
as i dedint hav nothing partikler to do.

i hadint gon out abov 2 miles or so,
when i sat down to rest by the rodside, & lo
A beautiful vishin burst fool on my ise,
which filld me with wundir & pleshur likwise.

On the opposeat side of the rod neeth a tree,
A luvly yung feemail sat stairing at me.
Her skin was like paypir, her ise they wir blak,
& her hare hung in ringlets $\frac{1}{2}$ way down her bak.

Oh many yung feemails ive sean in my time,
& a good feu ive red of in prose & in rime,
But i niver hav hard of, nor nivcr have seen
a made $\frac{1}{2}$ so fare, any place whair ive bean.

With a hop step & gump i flue into Her arms,
While i shouted deer angel oh ceese your alarms,
I meen you no harm, but i wish you to say
if your'e marrid or singel, kum tell me i pray.

she spok nut a wurd for a minnit or 2
Then she sed i wood like to no what's that to you.
oh nothing i kried, but if singel you are,
1 will wed you to-moro my beautyfool star.

Indeed, youre remarkably kind she replied,
But allow me to stait i already am tied.
Alas i exklaimd while i kissed her sweat face,
I'm exceedinglie soro that sutch is the kase.

But sumwhat astonished at me she did seam,
For she opened her mouth wide, & gave a loud skream,
Whitch brote a grate numbir of men on the sean,
who bald out you vagabon, what do you mean.

mi sole now was filled with strainge feers & alarms,
For they seasd me at wance by the legs & the arms
& marched me along to the brink of a pool,
and emptied me into its waters so kool.

The pool being shalo i fell with a thud,
& stuck neerly up to the neck among mud,
& at last when of life i had given up all hope,
the skowndrils took pity & threw me a rope.

with a desperit efort i droo myself out,
then they sadly abused me, and pushed me about,
But at lenth i got home fool of soro & pane,
Determined i niver wood kort thair again.

———o———

MARY'S NOO AWA.'

THE vaulted lift's a bonnie blue,
   The mornin' sun shines bricht,
The hills a' glisten, bathed wi' dew,
   And tinged wi' golden licht ;

Green leafy buds bloom freshly fair,
　　Dame Nature's buskin' braw;
Her charms delight my een nae mair,
　　For Mary's noo awa.'

The balmy spring winds, mild and saft,
　　Sigh o'er th' sunny sea,
And wantonly rich perfumes waft
　　Frae hawthorn hedge and lea,
Whaur snaw-white daisies, sweet blue-bells,
　　And pale primroses blaw:
To me their beauty only tells
　　O' Mary noo awa.'

Th' kine browse gladly by th' rills,
　　Th' lambs frisk o'er th' braes,
Th' laverock soarin' liftward trills
　　Its matin hymn o' praise,
Th' merle's mellow notes lood ring
　　Through briery dell and shaw,
But to my heart nae joy they bring,
　　For Mary's noo awa.'

Sae sad and pensively I stray,
　　While nature smiles sae sweet,
My lanely heart's sae dull an' wac
　　That whiles I'm like to greet.
Th' glories o' th' gladd'nin' scene
　　But memories reca'
O' happy days that ance hae been,
　　And Mary noo awa.'

———o———

THE SLIGHTED MAIDEN.

OH, tell me, dost thou love me now
   All truly and sincere?
'Twill ease my heart to know if thou
   Dost hold me still as dear
As when, beneath the rowan tree
   Far down the ferny dell,
With cheek to mine press'd, thou to me
   Love's story first didst tell?

I ask because methinks each time
   We meet more cold thou'rt grown;
And o'er thy face e'en now I trace
   A sullen silence thrown.
No more my presence seems to give
   Delight or joy to thee,
But all is sad, in shadow clad,
   Where sunshine used to be.

Thou dost not kiss me when we meet,
   Nor whisper loving words,
In soft low tones,—to me more sweet
   Than melody of birds,—
As thou wert wont in days bygone,
   When first with thee I met;
Thy love-star then so brightly shone,
   I could not think 'twould set.

I have been told—say, can it be?—
   Another now doth share
The love thou promised all to me,
   But the thought I cannot bear;

And yet the truth I long to know,
  Though my poor foolish heart
Should break. Oh, tell me, is it so?
  Thou'rt silent! must we part?

Where now are all the promises
  Thou solemnly didst make,
That I alone thy life should bless,
  That thou shouldst ne'er forsake
Me for another? But from this
  Farewell, false, fickle heart!
I would not rob thee of that bliss
  Another can impart.

———o———

BONNIE EDENSIDE.

THROUGH Cumbrian valleys to the sea
  Flows many a lovely stream,
But none among them all to me
  So fair and bright doth seem
As Eden dear, so cool and clear
  Its waters calmly glide;
To me there's not so dear a spot
  As bonnie Edenside.

For there I spent life's early hours
  In innocence and joy,
And played among the leafy bowers
  A happy, careless boy;
A youth love-dreaming I have strayed,
  And wooed and won my bride,
Among thy shades and mossy glades,
  Dear bonnie Edenside.

K

In idle hours I wander oft
  With rod in hand, to lure
The silvery trout, so shy, from out
  Thy pools and shallows pure.
Oh, then what rapture thrills my heart,
  How swift the moments glide,
By heathy fell and sylvan dell,
  On bonnie Edenside !   .

Since youth what changes I have seen,
  And cares have come to me !
But still, dear stream, my thoughts have been
  The same through all to thee.
And when life's weary task is o'er,
  Let death not us divide,
But let me sleep, I ask no more,
  Dear Eden, by thy side.

———0———

MAY MORNING AT THE MAINS.

WAKEN, waken early, merry lads and lasses,
Dew-drops fresh and pearly gleam o'er all the grasses ;
Ere the twilight shadows brighten into day,
To the dewy meadows gaily haste away.
Fling aside all sadness, banish care and pain,
Sing a song of gladness—May has come again !

Leave the lanes and alleys of the sickly city,
Hasten to the valleys, maidens young and pretty ;
Flowers have now unfolden, beautiful to view,
Their wee petals—golden, purple, pink, and blue.

FROM SPRING TO WINTER.

With a hey-down-derry, banish care and pain—
Radiant, rosy, merry May has come again !

.   .   .   .

Sol, with saffron glory, paints the hills and plains;
Now beside the hoary Castle of the Mains [1]
Many a blushing maiden and bright lad are seen,
On the cool, dew-laden, flower-bespangled green.
Some are merrily dancing ; others, blythe and gay,
Sing with notes entrancing, welcoming sweet May.

By the brooklet foaming down the rocky dell
Some are gladly roaming, loving tales to tell ;
Others, thoughtful, tarry, lingering to behold
Beauties, blue and starry, on the verdant wold;
Other groups are sitting in cool shady bowers,
Pretty chaplets knitting with the sweet wild-flowers.

Now a maiden stealeth slyly out of sight,
Blushing now she kneeleth 'mong the daises white :
Now her fair complexion bathes she with the dew,
To keep her colour rosy all the long year through.
Each and all are casting life's sad cares away—
May their joys be lasting, and aye sweet as May !

———o———

FROM SPRING TO WINTER.

In the gladsome hours of the sweet spring-time,
    We met, I remember, my love and I,
Under the shade of a blossoming lime,
    Under the blue of a cloudless sky.

[1] A famous resort for young people on May morning.

I touched her hand, and my being thrilled
  With a new desire and a strange delight,
While the flower-gemmed meadows and emerald hills
  Had never before seemed half so bright.

We wandered together, my love and I,
  Through leafy lanes, in the summer hours ;
The birds sang sweet in each green retreat,
  The bees were humming among the flowers.
But I do not think that the bees or the birds
  Were half so glad as my love and I,
When I asked her a question in love-born words,
  And 'Yes' was the tremulous, low reply.

In the golden prime of the autumn-time,
  With sunshine flushing the earth and sky,
My life was crowned with a joy sublime,
  We stood at the altar, my love and I.
I watched so proudly the love-light shine
  For me in her eyes, like a star in heaven,
And I thought that surely a bliss like mine
  Was never before to mortal given.

The snow lay white on the wintry wold ;
  I stood alone by a grassy mound,
Where slumbered my darling, so pale and cold,—
  O sorrowful hour ! O grief profound !
No matter how brightly the sun shines now,
  The earth and the sky look cold and grey ;
For love's soft light, that made all things bright,
  Is quenched with my hopes in the grave away.

———0———

LILY BELL.

FAR in a wild and lanely glen,
  Beside a burnie clear,
There stands a cosy but an' ben,
  Whaur lives a lassie dear ;
And oh, I loe that lassie mair
  Than words o' mine can tell !
She's artless, winsome, pure, and fair,
  My bonnie Lily Bell.

Madonna-like her features are,
  Fu' courteous is her mien ;
The love licht, like a trembling star,
  Glints in her dark-blue een ;
Her lips outvie the ruby coral,
  Her cheek the pink sea-shell,
Her teeth mair white than ony pearl,
  My bonnie Lily Bell.

Her hair is like the fleecy cluds
  The settin' sun shines through,
Her voice like merle's in the wuds
  When fa's the e'enin' dew ;
Her breath is sweet as May winds saft,
  Blawn through the hawthorn dell,
Whaur in the simmer gloamins aft
  I tryst dear Lily Bell.

Alang wi' her life's cares gie place
  To rosy, blissful dreams ;
And while I gaze in her sweet face,
  A paradise earth seems.

We've pledged our vows; should fate decree
　Our cherished hopes to quell,
The brichtest days were dark to me,
　My bonnie Lily Bell.

———o———

JANET SHAND.

WHAUR windin' Lochty wimples doon
　To mingle wi' the Leven clear,
And drumlie Ore a drowsy tune
　Hums to its castle ruins drear,
There blooms as fair a flower, I trow,
　As e'er by lover's een was scann'd ;
Eclipsed by nane, and match'd by few,
　Is dear kind-hearted Janet Shand.

Her velvet cheeks wear vermeil tints,
　Dark-broon her silken hair and een,
Wine-red her dewy lips, while glint
　Twin raws o' ivory teeth atween.
But a' her ootward charms combined
　My heart could never hae trepann'd,
If inward beauty o' the mind
　Had graced na gentle Janet Shand.

Lang pairted though we havena been,
　I feel as lanesome, dull, and wae,
As if her face I hadna seen
　For mony a lang and weary day.

To her by day my fancy turns,
  By nicht I dream that, hand in hand,
'Mang flow'ry braes, by crystal burns,
  I gaily roam wi' Janet Shand.

Speed on, ye langsome hours, and bring
  That happy day when to my heart
I'll fauld her 'neath love's downy wing,
  Nae mair on earth till death to part.
If wantin' her, though routh o' gear
  Were mine, wi' flunkies at command,
I'd gladly yield them a' to share
  Cauld puirtith's cup wi' Janet Shand.

———0———

THE DEAR OLD LAND.

AN exile on a foreign strand,
  Forlorn and sad I stray,
While dreaming of my fatherland,
  Full many a league away.
I muse on joys for ever fled, ·
  And friends I fondly cherish,
And sunny memories that ne'er
  Within my heart shall perish.
    The dear old land, the brave old land,
      The land of lake and river !
    Where'er I be, dear home, to thee
      My thoughts are turning ever.

Though vine-clad hills around me rise,
   And fertile valleys smile,
'Neath balmy, blue, unclouded skies,
   They never can beguile
My thoughts from Scotia's rocky glens,
   Her mountains grand and hoary,
Her solitudes, and streams, and woods,
   Renowned in song and story.
      The dear old land, etc.

Though fortune here has on me smiled,
   Yet still I sigh and pine
For pleasures wealth can never yield,
   And joys that once were mine ;—
The joys of childhood's sunny hours,
   And youth's bright dream,—love-laden,—
While roaming in the birken bowers
   With my sweet, dark-eyed maiden.
      The dear old land, etc.

How oft I gaze with wistful eyes
   Across the trackless foam,
Until I see in fancy rise
   The dear blue hills of home !
In spirit then I stray again
   Beside the Tay's clear river ;
My native home, where'er I roam,
   Forget thee I can never !
      The dear old land, etc.

———0———

MEET ME, LOVE.

ERE the crimson blush of the dying day
Grows pale where the sun hath sunk away,
  When the blue hills, veiled in purple mist,
  By the orange-tinted clouds are kissed.
'Neath the shady elm by the ruined tower,
Meet me, love, in that calm sweet hour.

Oh! then, whilst the balmy summer breeze
Wooingly whispers among the trees,
  We'll roam through the depths of the cool green dell,
  And gather the primrose and sweet blue-bell,
With the daisy, and cowslip, and lily fair,
A garland to weave round thy pale-brown hair.

And, love, with thee, what bliss will be mine !
To rest 'neath the shade of the green-hair'd pine,
  And hear the plaintive, soothing song
  Of the limpid brook as it leaps along,
While the blackbird carols its vesper hymn,
And the cushat coos in the woodland dim.

Then, love, while the sunset glories pale,
And the cawing rooks all homeward sail,
  When the shepherd has left the lonely hill,
  And the little bird and the bee are still,
When the dewy flowers fall fast asleep,
And the sweet-faced stars begin to peep
  From the violet sky, I will tell to thee
  How thou art dearer than all to me.

A HOPELESS LOVE.

FAREWELL ! dear friend, for so I'll call thee now ;
  Love's silver cord, which bound our hearts, is broken,
And golden dreams, like the day's transient bow,
  Have faded.   Fare thee well ! forget we've spoken ;
But oh, 'twere better we had never met !
'Tis easier to remember than forget.

We met,—'twas but to love ; and now we part,—
  'Tis for thy good.   Think not of me unkindly :
Thine image on the mirror of my heart
  Is fixed ; my fault is having loved too blindly.
Oh, love so hopeless ! dreamings all so vain !
I dare not ask to look on thee again.

I'm leaving thee for ever ; none may tell
  Of my deep grief ; forget thee I can never ;
Thy memory within my soul shall dwell,
  A golden sun-gleam on life's dark rough river.
The joyous hours we've spent—too bright to last—
I'll cherish,—sunniest memories of the past !

Banish for ever from thy pure young mind
  All thoughts of one who is unworthy of thee ;
Forget the shadowed past.   Thou yet shalt find
  A nobler soul to cherish and to love thee,
A heart more worthy such a love as thine,—
Thou merit'st even a holier love than mine.

Farewell ! may God watch o'er thee evermore,
  While on thy voyage across life's solemn ocean,

And bring thee safely to the peaceful shore,
  Safe from the world's wild tumult and commotion,
Where earthly toils and cares and sorrows cease,
Where's nought but purest joy, serenest peace !

———o———

THE LOVERS' PARTING.

WEEP not though I leave thee,
I will ne'er deceive thee,
, Let the thought not grieve thee,
          Nor in thy bosom dwell.

Distance, darling, never
Can our fond hearts sever ;
Love pure as the river
          Absence cannot quell.

Mutual vows we've spoken,
Pledged ne'er to be broken,
By a simple token,
          Ah ! so dear to me.

Life were void of pleasure,
Wanting thee, my treasure ;
Bliss beyond all measure
          Mine alone with thee.

But when we are parted,
Lone and sorrow hearted,
Present joys all thwarted,
          Time will yet renew.

Let no false fears move thee,
Only think I love thee
As the stars above thee,
        Faithful, pure, and true.

Beauty as divine, love,
Eyes that softly shine, love,
Sweetly blue as thine, love,
        Still may smile on me,

Only to recall, love,
Thine more dear than all, love ;
Whatsoe'er befall, love
        I'll be true to thee.

———o———

THE LOVERS' MEETING.

AND do I hold thee in mine arms, my treasure, once again !
Now vanished all my heart's alarms, and all its fears now
        vain,
The fears that absent years might blot my memory from
        thy mind,
Or that thou mightest have forgot the vows our hearts that
        bind!

I've come to find thee true as when, all tearfully, we took
A long farewell down in the den beside the tiny brook ;
The sacred vows we uttered then live changeless in my
        heart,
And we shall pledge them o'er again that ne'er till death
        we part.

'hy warm soft cheek again I kiss, 'tis wet with joyous tears ;
'h, how my heart hath longed for this through all these
   long sad years !
ly heart's deep fountains overflow with purest joy's excess,
;lad thoughts within my bosom glow that words cannot
   express !

———*0*———

SWEET DREAMS OF HOME.

'NEATH a still and starry sky
   Bounds our good ship o'er the foam ;
Lonely on the deck I lie,
      Far, far from home.
Musing on life's toils and woes,
   Wearily mine eyelids close;
Now I sink in calm repose,
      Dreaming of home.

Once again I gladly stray
   By the calm bright silver Tay,
Where I spent youth's joyous day,
      Dear native home !
Rise before me heather hills,
   Briery dells and crystal rills,
Oh, my soul with rapture fills !
      Dreaming of home.

Many years I've passed since then,
   Sailing o'er life's trackless foam,
But youth's joys come back again,
      Dreaming of home.

Rosy visions, blissful dreams,
  Oh ! ye come like golden gleams,
Lighting life's dark troubled streams,
  Sweet dreams of home !

————o————

LILY.

FAR away the stars are beaming
  In the blue and silent sky,
While I wander lonely, dreaming
  Over happy days gone by,—
Over golden hours departed,
  When thy smile was life to me ;
Oh, I'm nearly broken hearted
  Since I parted, love, from thee !

Darling, all day long I miss thee,
  Miss thy kindly voice and smile ;
Oh, could I but once more kiss thee,
  All my grief it would beguile !
Life seemed all a dream of gladness,
  Lily love, when thou wert near ;
Now my heart is full of sadness,
  And the days seem long and drear.

Autumn winds are sadly sighing,
  Autumn flowers all sadly wave
O'er thy silent form, now lying
  In the dark and lonesome grave.
Oh, I long to be beside thee,
  Free from earthly care and pain,
Since the star that used to guide me
  Ne'er on me will shine again !

MARY, THE MAID O' DUNDEE.

THE dim purple shades o' th' twilight are creepin'
    In silence o'er mountain, vale, muirlan', an' rill,
Th' gloamin' star doon frae th' blue lift is keekin',
    Th' yellow moon glow'rs o'er yon heather-croon'd hill ;
Its pale gowden glimmer is tingin' sae clearly
    Th' Tay's ripplin' waves whaur they wed wi' the sea,
As joyfu' I haste to meet ane I loe dearly,
    My ain bonnie Mary, th' Maid o' Dundee.

Th' blue-bell an' primrose th' green wilds adornin'
    Nae fairer or purer, I trow, are than she ;
Her smiles are as blythe as the first beams o' mornin',
    She's meek as th' daisy that gems th' green lea ;
Her kind heart is true as the stars that are blinkin'
    Far up the wide welkin, dark-blue as her e'e.
By nicht I'm aye dreamin', by day I'm aye thinkin',
    O' Mary, dear Mary, the Maid o' Dundee.

O' a' earthly pleasures, there's nane that sae dearly
    I prize as to meet, in th' calm gloamin' hour,
The bonnie sweet lassie I loe sae sincerely,
    And rest in th' shade o' some green leafy bower.
For, oh, then what rapture, our tale o' love tellin' !
    Th' world's wealth couldna sic happiness gie ;
Oh, brichtly th' love-star will halo th' dwellin'
    O' me and dear Mary, th' Maid o' Dundee !

—————0————

.